THE BLACKGAARD CHRONICLES™

BOOK TWO
PAWN'S PLAY

PHIL LOLLAR

FOCUS ON THE FAMILY.

The Blackgaard Chronicles: *Pawn's Play*

© 2017 Focus on the Family. All rights reserved.

This book is based on Adventures in Odyssey audio drama episodes "Connie Goes to Camp, Part 1"; "Connie Goes to Camp, Part 2"; and "Eugene's Dilemma"—original scripts by Paul McCusker.

Novelization by Phil Lollar

Cover design by Jacob Isom
Cover illustration by Gary Locke

For Library of Congress Cataloging-in-Publication Data for this title, visit http://www.loc.gov/help/contact-general.html.

ISBN: 978-1-58997-927-7

Printed in the United States of America

23   22   21   20   19   18   17
7   6   5   4   3   2   1

For
Nathan Carlson
and
Will Ryan

Don't miss *Opening Moves*, Book 1 in The Blackgaard Chronicles book series. Available from better bookstores everywhere and at www.WhitsEnd.org/Store.

The Blackgaard Chronicles are based on popular Adventures in Odyssey (AIO) audio drama series. Learn more at www.aioclub.org, including how to get access to the complete library of AIO episodes, exclusive AIO radio dramas, daily devotions, and much more.

CHAPTER ONE

Summer 1989 . . .

R ichard Maxwell was sweating.

A lot.

Despite the cool air in his present location—
wherever it was—sweat beaded on his forehead and
upper lip and trickled down his back, soaking his shirt.
He had obviously messed up somewhere. But how? He

was certain he had accounted for all the variables. No one could have known. He didn't make any mistakes.

Or so he thought until a few hours ago. That's when he realized how wrong he was.

Was it a few hours ago? It could have been longer. It was hard to tell time in the back of a sealed-up van with no windows or lights.

It was like something out of a bad movie: he was walking home from his job at the retirement home, having just stolen what promised to be his best haul yet, when the van pulled up alongside him, and two beefy guys manhandled him into the back. They slid the door shut, and the van took off so fast, he tumbled to the rear and banged his head against the back door.

They drove for what seemed like a long time, and when they finally stopped and opened the door, he was surprised to see they were in what he assumed was a nearly empty warehouse. The only things in it were the van and a small table with two chairs framed in a pool of light from the ceiling. The beefy guys pulled him out of the van and sat him down in one of the chairs. One of them placed the backpack of pilfered items on the table, and then they both turned and left, their footsteps echoing in the darkness.

A man with pasty skin, thinning salt-and-pepper hair, a potbelly, and milky gray eyes sat in the chair opposite Maxwell, looking at the contents of a file folder. The angle of the light caused his hooked nose to cast a strange shadow across his mouth and chin.

Without looking up, the man said, "Richard Maxwell: janitor, con artist, swindler, manipulator, and now—" He set down the folder and upended the backpack. The contents of the day's haul spilled out onto the table. The man smirked at him. "—petty thief. My, my, you've led quite a life for someone so young, haven't you?"

Maxwell thought there was something familiar about this jerk; he'd seen him somewhere. Then it hit him. "I know you. You're like a city-government guy from Odyssey, right?"

The man smiled a greasy sort of smile. "Not *like*. *Am*. Councilman Philip Glossman. I wish I could say I was pleased to make your acquaintance. But I'm not."

Maxwell licked his lips nervously. "Look, I . . . I was just holding that stuff for a friend."

Glossman held up a finger and wagged it, pursing his lips and shaking his head slightly. "Please. Don't even try."

This was weird, Maxwell thought. Since when could city councilmen arrest people? And why all the subterfuge? He fought to stay cool. "So . . . where am I? What is this place?"

"All in good time, Maxwell. All in good time." Glossman examined the contents of the backpack. He picked up a gold brooch shaped like a butterfly. Tiny, sparkling diamonds lined its wings. "Pretty." He smirked. "Though it doesn't really go with your outfit."

That was it. Maxwell slammed his hands on the

table and jumped up. "What is this? What's going on here?"

Glossman continued smirking. "Sit down, Maxwell," he said evenly.

Maxwell leaned across the table. "I've got rights! You can't arrest me without telling me why."

Glossman laughed. "Who said you've been arrested?"

Maxwell leaned back slowly and swallowed hard. "If you're not arresting me, then—" He sank down in the chair, heart pounding. "Y-you . . . you're . . . kidnapping me?"

A bigger laugh. "Hardly! Why kidnap someone nobody would pay a ransom for?"

"Then what's going on?" Maxwell's voice was almost pleading. "Why did you bring me here?"

Glossman scooted back his chair, stood, and stepped behind it. "I've brought you here to meet someone—someone who very much wants to meet you." He turned his head and called into the darkness behind him. "Sir!"

After a few moments, Maxwell heard a door open,

though he saw no light. The door closed, and one set of footsteps, accompanied by the occasional tap-tap of a walking stick, echoed in the empty building. The footsteps and the walking stick were headed right toward him and grew louder with each step and tap.

Suddenly another man appeared in the pool of light. He was tall and lean, with angular features. He wore a black, three-piece suit, tailored to fit him perfectly. The coat fell almost to his knees, the trousers were sharply creased, and his black shoes were polished to a high gloss. He carried a black walking stick with a polished gold knob for a handle. His hair was jet black, save for white streaks that ran from both temples to the back of his head on both sides, and his mustache and Vandyke beard were also jet black.

Glossman held out the chair for the man, and he glided into it with an easy grace, placing his walking stick on the table atop the pilfered loot. He looked across the table and smiled, teeth gleaming, and his gaze sent chills down Maxwell's spine.

"Hello, Richard." The man's voice was deep, dark,

rich, and cold as ice. "I'm Dr. Regis Blackgaard. You and I need to talk."

Maxwell took steady, even breaths, though his heart was pounding. As casually as he could, he reached up and wiped the sweat from his brow and upper lip. "Okaaaay," he said. He was surprised how calm his voice sounded. "So . . . let's talk."

Blackgaard smiled pleasantly but said nothing, so Maxwell continued. "Uh . . . nice weather we're having? Great place you got here? How about them Cubs? Whadaya wanna talk about?"

"Why, about *you*, of course, Richard." Blackgaard's smile widened. "More specifically, about your future."

Maxwell took a deep breath. "O-okay, look, I-I admit to taking a few trinkets from the geezers, okay? But I got your message. I won't do it again. You don't have to threaten me!"

Blackgaard's brow furrowed. "Threaten? Are you under the impression that I've brought you here to harm you?"

Maxwell blinked, then swallowed. "Well . . . uh . . .

yeah . . . sort of. I mean, when you have two thugs grab me off the street and throw me in the back of a van—"

Blackgaard shook his head. "That was for your safety! Those men were there to protect you."

"Protect me from *who*?"

"Now, Richard," said Blackgaard reprovingly. "Don't be so naive. Surely you realize that your past actions have made you more than a few enemies. My men had your best interests at heart, I assure you."

"Then why are you keeping me here against my will?"

"Am I?" Blackgaard shook his head again. "I think you've completely misconstrued the situation. You're free to leave whenever you like."

Now Maxwell's brow furrowed. Who *was* this guy? "W-well if you're not gonna hurt me, and you're not holding me, then why *am* I here?"

"I'd have thought that would be obvious by now," Blackgaard said, smiling again. "I want to hire you."

Maxwell's jaw dropped. "*Hire* me? B-b-but I . . . you . . . he . . . *what*?"

Blackgaard laughed. "My, my, this is a jolly

mix-up!" He looked up at Glossman, who joined him in laughter.

Maxwell wasn't laughing. These guys were nuts! "If all you wanted to do was offer me a job, then why the big production—the blacked-out van, the long ride, the dark warehouse, the spotlight?"

Blackgaard rose from his chair. "I'm so very sorry, Richard," he said in a sincere tone. "I understand now how all this must appear to you. My associate here"— he nodded at Glossman—"has a tendency to be, shall we say, overly dramatic in his actions on occasion."

Maxwell looked at Glossman, who smirked and shrugged. Blackgaard slowly moved around the table to Maxwell's side. "Thus, the blacked-out van. This warehouse is near the airport I happen to own. I have a very busy travel schedule. In fact, I'll be catching a flight out shortly, so it was the most convenient place and time for us to meet—which is why you had such a long ride here. Again, I'm sorry for that. As for the lights, I just feel it's a terrible waste of energy to turn them all on when it's just the three of us in here. I can do so if you like, though—if it will make you more comfortable." Blackgaard was standing next to him now, practically over him.

"No . . . that's okay." *It all sounds so reasonable*, Maxwell thought. *So why does this still give me the creeps?* He took another breath, then said aloud, "Look, Mr. Blackgaard—"

"Doctor."

"Huh?"

"*Dr.* Regis Blackgaard." He smiled again, but his eyes were cold. "PhD in psychology."

"Oh, uh, sorry, uh . . . *Dr.* Blackgaard, I'm still pretty confused here. You said you know about my past—about the things I've, uh, supposedly done."

Blackgaard chuckled. "Well put."

"But you still want to hire me?"

"Indeed." Blackgaard nodded. "In fact, your past is *why* I want to hire you."

Maxwell blinked again. "Okay, I just went from pretty confused to totally confused."

Blackgaard sat on the edge of the table. "Richard,

most people who looked at your . . . résumé would no doubt see precisely what Mr. Glossman saw: con artist, swindler, manipulator, petty thief. But do you know what I see?"

"What?"

Blackgaard leaned in slightly. "An entrepreneur— resourceful, clever, intelligent. An energetic young man who is willing to do whatever it takes to get ahead. I want a young man like that on my team."

"You do."

"Oh yes. I want to help you, Richard."

Maxwell's eyes narrowed. "Why?"

Blackgaard sat back. "An excellent question. The answer is, because I believe that you can also help me."

Maxwell smirked. "And there it is. The other shoe."

"Other shoe? I'm afraid I don't—"

"Stop with the innocent routine already!" Maxwell leaned back, put his foot on the table, tilted his chair on its two back legs, and intertwined his fingers behind his head. "You want something from me. Something you can't do . . . something you want bad enough to bring me all the way here, flatter me, and bribe me with a job to get it. So why don't you just tell me what it is?"

Glossman's eyes were wide. Blackgaard stood and walked back around the table. Glossman held out the chair for him, but Blackgaard didn't sit. Instead, he stopped, faced Maxwell, focused his coal-black eyes directly on him . . . and laughed. "You have a lot more spunk than I gave you credit for, Richard. Very well. You're enrolled at Campbell College, correct?"

"Yeah."

"Majoring in computer science?"

"Two for two."

"I need a computer expert."

Maxwell grinned. "I figured. To do what?"

Blackgaard sat. "I believe it's called hacking—using a computer at one location to break into another computer at a different location."

"Yeah." Maxwell nodded. "I'm familiar with the term."

"Can you do it?"

Maxwell took his hands from behind his head. "Maybe. If I have a powerful enough computer hooked up to a modem." He quickly decided not to mention that the other computer had to be hooked up to a modem as well. He learned long ago to always leave himself a plausible excuse for failure. Besides, he now had an idea of where this was going, and he had his own scheme in mind.

Blackgaard leaned forward. "Like the computers at Campbell College?"

Maxwell took his foot off the table. The chair jolted forward onto all four legs. "Not the lab computers." He thought for a moment. "I'd need to use the one in the computer security room."

Blackgaard licked his lips. "Can you get to it?"

"Did you miss the part where I said it was a *security* room? The place is locked up tighter than a drum."

Blackgaard exhaled and sat back in his chair.

Glossman tugged at his collar and eyed Blackgaard with a wary look.

Apparently the good doctor here doesn't like disappointment, Maxwell thought. He smirked and said aloud, "But as it turns out, the college just happens to be looking for an entrepreneurial, resourceful, clever, intelligent, energetic computer-science major to head up its high-security programming section—in the computer security room."

Glossman stopped tugging at his collar and scowled at Maxwell.

Blackgaard leaned forward again. "Excellent!" He fixed his coal-black eyes on Maxwell. "I meant what I said, Richard. I want you on my team. Can I count on you?"

Maxwell shrugged. "I dunno. What's in it for me—besides a lousy job, I mean?"

"What every entrepreneurial, resourceful, clever, intelligent, energetic young person wants." Blackgaard's voice lowered to a near whisper. "Power." His eyes bored into Maxwell's. "What do you say?"

Maxwell leaned back in his chair again. "Whose computer do you want me to hack into?"

Blackgaard exchanged a look with Glossman and then smiled at Maxwell. "Have you ever heard of a place called . . . Whit's End?"

CHAPTER TWO

Dear Mom,

I'm sorry it's taken me so long to write you a letter, but you know how crazy it is here at Camp What-A-Nut. Especially since they made me a girls' cabin counselor.

How's everything in Odyssey? Have you seen Whit? Or Eugene? It feels so strange not working at Whit's End, and the past few days up here haven't made those feelings go away. If anything, it's made them worse, because a lot of the kids who went to Whit's End are up here and know I was fired. So now every time I look at them, I feel embarrassed and hurt—and angry. It just doesn't seem right that Whit would fire me over a silly computer program.

But being busy is better than sitting at home all day. It was "hit the ground running" right from the start. As soon as everybody checked in, we all gathered together in the great hall—which is also the cafeteria and the chapel—for the camp director's welcome speech. He told us all about the camp's history and how it got its weird name. Its real name is Camp Wey-Aka-Tal-Ah-Nee-Tee, a Native American phrase that supposedly means "land that stinks like swamp." But that took too long to say, and no one could pronounce it right when they *did* say it. So they took the first letters—W-A-T-A-N-T—and, well, someone said it looked like "what-a-nut," and—voilà!—Camp What-A-Nut was born.

After his speech, I gathered the girls in my cabin together in a corner of the meeting hall to go over the

rules. I think you know most of them from church
(the girls, I mean, not the rules): Lucy Cunningham-Schultz, Donna Barclay, Robyn Jacobs—and one
you don't know, Alison Leskowsky. She used to come
to Whit's End. You wouldn't have any trouble picking
out my girls among all the kids here, even if you didn't
know them: Lucy has brown hair (and glasses), Donna
has dark hair and blue eyes, Robyn has red hair and
freckles, and Alison is a blonde with a slight overbite.
They all pretty much always hang out together, so all
I have to do is look for a group of girls that consists of
one brown, one black, one red, and one blonde head,
and I've found them.

The rules were pretty standard safety stuff: no sports
activities in the cabins; the beds are not trampolines,
and the pillows are not clubs; and no food allowed outside the cafeteria, especially not in the cabins, because
it attracts raccoons, opossums, skunks, and bears. And
most important: campers are not allowed outside after
lights out. I told them that one is the biggie. Break it,
and you could get sent home. Even though this camp

isn't exactly roughing it, it's still out in the wilderness, which means you can still run into danger. I remember hearing about Donny McCoy last year, when a bear chased him and . . . well . . . someone up a tree.

Oh, who am I kidding? It was *Whit* who named the camp and Whit who was chased up the tree! Even when I'm trying to avoid talking about him, I can't avoid talking about him. I know it was my fault I got fired—and got Eugene fired too. I know I disobeyed Whit, and I know how disappointed he was in me. But I told him I was sorry, and I really *am*! I just don't understand. Whit told me that Christianity is all about forgiveness, that no matter how many times we may do something bad, God forgives us when we ask Him to. So why won't Whit forgive me now?

I guess even with being busy here at camp, it's still going to take time to get over this, right?

I'm sorry I'm complaining. I need to be more like Lucy. All of the other girls in my cabin have been cranky for one reason or another almost since they got here—either about not being able to watch TV (Alison) or getting their clothes dirty (Robyn) or smearing their makeup (Donna) or wanting to do what the boys do (Alison, Robyn, and Donna).

The only one who hasn't complained is Lucy. But then again, Lucy never complains. She's very sweet and always does what she's supposed to do. Lucy even managed to make a new friend in craft class: Jill Blankenship. Her uncle is Charley Blankenship, the camp caretaker. He's a short, round guy who rides around on a little tractor and spits tobacco juice everywhere, but he's likable enough, and he does keep the camp in shipshape. I heard Jill tell Lucy that thanks to Uncle Charley, she knows the camp like the back of her hand—all of the secret paths and hideouts. If Jill was talking to anyone but Lucy, that might make me nervous, like they were up to something. But I know Lucy has a good head on her shoulders.

Well, Mom, I need to go. We're going on our first nature walk/campout tomorrow—where we stay out in tents for a couple of nights—and I need to pack my backpack for it. It should be a lot of fun, if I can get the girls to pay attention to nature instead of their hair and nails and what activities the boys are doing.

Write back soon! If you see Eugene, tell him to write me too! And please pray for me, that I can have some peace about Whit.

Love,

Connie

CHAPTER THREE

"Good grief! It *still* stinks like him!"

Philip Glossman pressed the autocontrol buttons for his car windows as he pulled out of the car wash driveway, rolling them all down simultaneously. He had been back in Odyssey from the Maxwell trip to the Chicago warehouse for three days now. His car had been sanitized inside three times, and it *still* smelled like Maxwell's cheap cologne. It was bad enough that

Blackgaard insisted Glossman give the punk kid a ride back to Odyssey. But now he had to put up with *this*?

"The gift that keeps on giving," he muttered, sticking his ski-slope nose out the window for a breath of fresh air. "I'm gonna have to sell this thing!"

The smell also served as a constant and gloomy reminder that the warehouse meeting did not end well for him. Once Maxwell was out of the room, Blackgaard asked for a progress report on procuring a new building for him in Odyssey. Glossman had found the perfect one: the old Gower's Landing shopping complex. It was the right size, was in a decent part of town, and had a good line of sight to Whit's End. Best of all, the complex was already half empty; for some reason, a lot of the shops that opened there just couldn't seem to turn a profit, and they soon closed down or moved. Over the years the complex developed a reputation for being bad for business.

Local folklore said it was because the original land-owner, Old Man Gower, was swindled out of the land and cursed the property so no one would ever make money on it. It was superstitious nonsense, of course, but useful information, as it made it a breeze for Webster Development to acquire the property. Once it had been acquired, the remaining tenants were more than happy to have Webster buy out their leases—with a small bonus and a promise of helping them find locations better for business.

That is, all the tenants except one.

Mansfield Computers. Its namesake and founder, Bob Mansfield, started the company three years ago. It was the only store in the Gower's Landing complex not just making money but good money. The booming home-computer market seemed to be curse-proof. Business was so good, in fact, that Mansfield refused Webster's offer.

Needless to say, when Glossman told Blackgaard that news, Blackgaard was not pleased.

Blackgaard's voice remained calm, but his coal-black eyes bored into Glossman's. "Do I have anything to be concerned about with this, Philip?"

"No, sir."

"You understand I need the entire building for what I have planned?"

"Yes, sir."

"Then I suggest you take a different approach with Mr. Mansfield."

"Different approach, sir?"

"Turn up the pressure. You've dangled the carrot before him, and he has rejected it. Now it's time for the whip. If Mr. Mansfield won't accept my generosity, then he will suffer my displeasure."

"What kind of displeasure did you have in mind?"

"I'm sure you and Webster can think of something."

"Yes, sir."

"I can count on you to do this, can't I, Philip?"

"Of course! Absolutely!"

"I certainly hope so."

Before he and Maxwell left the warehouse for Odyssey, Glossman called Webster Development to convey Blackgaard's displeasure and relay his orders. It always amused Glossman that Webster Development was actually just one man named Holden Webster, a short, pudgy, balding, doughy-skinned chum of Glossman's from college, who had even fewer scruples than Glossman did, and almost as few as Blackgaard.

Webster immediately came up with several ideas for making Mansfield's business more difficult: tripling the lease, tacking on surcharges for electricity, and hitting him with various code violations. Glossman approved them all, and Webster promised to implement them immediately. Today was Glossman's first chance to check on the situation, and the Gower's Landing complex was the next stop on his itinerary.

Glossman fully expected to see the store dark, with moving trucks outside. But as he pulled in front of the complex, he slowed his car to a crawl. The parking lot was nearly full, and people were fairly swarming to get into Mansfield Computers.

Glossman fought the panicked feeling rising in his chest. *Don't jump to conclusions,* he thought. *Maybe this is a going-out-of-business sale.* He turned into the lot and drove up the main aisle toward the store.

That's when he saw it.

A huge banner hung over the front door of Mansfield Computers. It read "Big sale! Must move old inventory for new inventory! Make us an offer!"

New inventory? Why would someone who should be moving out order new inventory? Glossman still fought the panic rising inside him. It was possible that Mansfield was ordering new inventory for his new location, but Glossman saw nothing on the banner or in the store windows that indicated Mansfield was moving. He decided to go inside and see for himself. He parked his car, rolled up the windows—leaving them open a crack in the hope that fresh air would replace the stench of cologne—locked the doors, and crossed the lot to the entrance.

Inside, the place was a near madhouse. People were everywhere—in every aisle, nook, and cranny of the store. The three cash registers had lines five and six people deep, all buying personal computers and other electronic devices.

Glossman knew he couldn't talk to Mansfield directly. Webster was the front man. So where was Webster? He needed to call the rotund little twerp. He headed for the door but stopped when he saw a familiar face. The face belonged to a skinny redhead with glasses and hair in his eyes. (How did he see through all that hair?) As usual, he wore jeans, a T-shirt, and a vest.

It was Eugene Meltsner.

One of Whittaker's former employees, thought Glossman. Eugene was looking down at some papers and not really paying attention to where he was going. Glossman altered his route and headed straight at him.

"Ooof!"

Eugene's papers went flying everywhere. "Oh dear!" Glossman exclaimed in feigned surprise. "I'm so sorry!"

"That's quite all right," Eugene responded, and as he started to retrieve his papers, he glanced at Glossman, did a double take worthy of a cartoon character, and then stopped. "Councilman Glossman?"

Glossman kept up his pretense of surprise. "Yes, I didn't see you, and I—Wait. You look familiar. Have we met?"

Eugene stiffened. "Not formally. I'm Eugene Meltsner. I've attended some of your town-council meetings."

"Yes! That's it! With Whittaker, right?"

Eugene's eyes dropped. "Uh, yes . . . er, correct."

"Is he here too? I'd like to talk to him."

"Uh, no, I don't believe so . . . That is, I don't really know." He sniffed, scowled slightly, then continued. "What I mean is, if Mr. Whittaker is here, then we're not here together." He sniffed again, scowled more deeply, and then bent down to retrieve his papers.

Glossman bent down with him. "Here, let me help you with that."

"No, it really isn't necessary—"

"It's the least I can do! I ran into you and—" Glossman stopped and held up one of the papers. "Application for employment?"

"I'll take that," Eugene snapped, looking extremely embarrassed. He plucked the paper from Glossman's hand.

This is getting fun, thought Glossman. *Look at him*

squirm. Aloud he said, "Does Whittaker know you want to moonlight on him?"

Eugene straightened his papers. "I'm not moonlighting." He stood, and so did Glossman. "I no longer work for Mr. Whittaker."

"Really?" said Glossman, feigning surprise again. "How come?" He could barely conceal his glee at how uncomfortable Eugene looked.

"If you don't mind, I'd rather not discuss it."

"Oh! Right! Sorry! I didn't mean to pry." Glossman gave a little headshake. "It's just that . . . you were quite a fixture over at Whit's End."

Eugene sighed deeply. "Yes, well, no longer."

Glossman leaned in slightly. "No offense, but isn't working at a computer store a little . . . well . . . beneath you?"

Eugene stiffened again. "There may have been a time when I thought so, but I have since learned that no honest job is beneath an honest person."

Glossman chuckled. "You sound like Whittaker."

"I'll take that as a compliment. Now, if you'll excuse me." Eugene started to turn, but Glossman stopped him.

"As I said, Eugene, I didn't mean any offense. Listen, I'm gonna do you a favor. You're a student at the college, right?"

"A graduate student, yes."

"And you obviously know about computers, or you wouldn't be applying here, right?"

Eugene nodded. "Computers are an expertise of mine, yes."

Glossman leaned in again. "Well, I happen to know that the college's computer department is hiring, and I also know the guy who is on the fast track to getting the supervisor's job. I could put in a good word for you if you want. Maybe even get you an introduction?"

Eugene studied him for a moment, looking unsure. Then he cleared his throat and said, "Well . . . uh . . . thank you, Councilman Glossman. That's very generous of you, but I must decline."

Glossman blinked. "Are you sure?"

Eugene took a deep breath and nodded slowly. "Yes . . . I'm quite sure. Thank you again, but no thanks."

Glossman shrugged. "Suit yourself. But if you change your mind, just give me a call at my office."

"Yes. Of course." Eugene nodded again. "Well, I really need to be going. Good-bye."

"Good-bye, Eugene."

Eugene turned and exited the store. Glossman watched him disappear into the parking lot. He had no idea why he'd just offered to help the kid, except that it was something Lizzy would have wanted him to do. He remembered her telling him once that people have a duty to help others when they can. He reached into his coat pocket and ran his fingers over the pocket watch she gave him with her picture in it. Yes, his lost love was the only person who brought out the best in him. She would want him to help Eugene.

He suddenly yanked his hand out of his pocket. Best not to have those thoughts. *Best to keep your mind on what you're doing.*

Besides, he just came up with another reason to

help Meltsner: gathering allies. It'd be smart to have someone like Eugene beholden to him. He looked around, suspicious. Yes, this was a time for forming alliances. He had a feeling he was going to need them.

He made his way to a pay phone in a corner of the store, lifted the receiver, paid, and dialed. The phone rang once, twice, thrice, and then clicked, and a recording of Webster's pompous voice said, "Hi! You've reached the Webster Development Firm. Your call is important to us. Please leave your name and number at the beep." The machine beeped, and Glossman said, "Holden, it's Philip. I'm at Mansfield Computers, and the place is buzzing. We need to talk. Where are you?"

"I'm right here."

Glossman started, then turned. Standing there was a squat, round man, with a bad comb-over of a few strands of dark hair and a five-o'clock shadow. He wore a Hawaiian shirt with a palm tree and pineapple pattern on it, Bermuda shorts, huarache sandals, and sunglasses perched on a pug nose. The Hawaiian shirt had barbecue stains down the front, which Glossman could barely see over the shopping cart filled with computers and computer parts that Webster was pushing.

Glossman hung up his phone. "Holden, what in the world are you doing?"

"What's it look like I'm doin'? I'm shoppin'!"

Glossman rounded the cart and grabbed Webster's arm. "Let's go," he muttered through gritted teeth. "Outside."

Webster yanked his arm away. "Hey, hey, hey! Not without my stuff! C'mon, you can help me take it to my car. I'm parked right out front."

Glossman took a deep breath, then gripped the front of the cart and pulled it out the exit while Webster pushed. True to his word, Webster's old jalopy was in a primo spot directly across from the entrance. Webster popped the trunk lid and started loading his purchases.

Glossman seethed. "Are you out of your mind? We're supposed to be putting this guy *out* of business, not helping him stay *in*!"

Webster nodded and shrugged. "I know, but you would not believe the deals this guy is offering!"

"Holden—"

"Look, I tried, all right? I threw every single idea I had at him."

"*None* of them worked?"

Webster shook his head. "I told him we were tripling his lease payments, and he produced an ironclad lease agreement that says we can't do that for three years."

"We can't wait three years."

"Tell me somethin' I *don't* know."

"What about the electricity? The surcharges—"

Webster sneered. "He's makin' so much money, he doesn't *care* about them."

"Then raise them even higher. Come up with more!"

"We can't. We've gone as far as we can legally go." Webster stuffed the last of the boxes into his trunk, closed the lid, and took a couple of short sniffs. "What is that *smell*?"

"What smell?"

"Cheap cologne."

Glossman sniffed himself. *Oh, man! It's on* me *now!* Aloud he said, "Never mind the smell. Are you sure there's nothing else we can do?"

Webster walked to his car door. "Positive." He unlocked the door and pulled it open. "Sorry, but if you want this guy outta here, you're gonna have to do it some other way. Now if you'll excuse me, I have computers to set up!" He jumped into his jalopy, closed the door, started her up, and sped off.

Glossman stewed in anger and rank-smelling cologne. He had no building, no way to get the building, and no good news for Blackgaard. And to top it all off, he was going to have to sell his car and burn his clothes because they smelled like Richard Maxwell.

This was not a good day.

CHAPTER FOUR

In the week that had passed since his warehouse en-
counter with Dr. Blackgaard, Richard Maxwell had
been quite busy. The day following his return to Odyssey, he went first thing to the Campbell College
Information Technology Department and applied for
the head of computer security position. Two geek-a-
zoids were also there applying; Maxwell recognized
them from his classes and was sure he knew more than
they did about computers.

According to the department secretary, no one else had applied, so he felt pretty confident going into the preliminary interview with the department head, Mr. Burglemeister. He was one of Maxwell's professors, and the preliminary interview went very well. Burglemeister was a bumbling old coot with a mop of wild gray hair and tiny spectacles perched on a pointed nose. His large belly seemed to arrive several seconds before he did, and he never got anyone's name right, including Maxwell's. Fortunately he liked to laugh, so Maxwell turned on the funny and the charm.

Burglemeister was all but eating out of his hand by the time the interview was over. "I vill haf a decision for you by Thursday, Maxstone," he said in his German-tinged accent.

"*Well*."

"Vell vat?"

"That's my name, sir. Max*well*."

Burglemeister roared with laughter and slapped Maxwell on the back. "You und your jokes! Very amusing!" He shuffled Maxwell out of the room and closed the door, still laughing.

Maxwell shook his head and smirked. *This is in the bag!*

As he walked across the quad after the interview, he thought about what he was getting himself into. Blackgaard was obviously a guy with resources and the will to use them. He not only had Glossman under his thumb—a town-council member with the pull to get Maxwell's records—but he also had other assets in and outside Odyssey, assets that were impressive, concerning, and cool.

On the impressive side, Blackgaard knew about an important computer program that Whittaker made called Applesauce, and the fact that Blackgaard knew about the program in the first place was especially impressive. Though Blackgaard didn't reveal how he knew about it, or exactly what it did, he did let slip (or was it on purpose?) that it was of interest to people at the highest levels of government. He also knew it had been used at least once at Whit's End, which ended up shutting down the place—zapping all of its electrical power—and getting a couple of employees fired.

Just how Blackgaard knew about the shutdown and firings was the concerning part. It seems another one of his operatives had actually been spying on Whit's End when Applesauce was used. He heard the employees yelling about it and was listening at the door when they got fired. That operative was Myron—aka Jellyfish—the very person through whom Maxwell had been fencing his stolen goodies from the old geezers at the Odyssey Retirement Home. Blackgaard told Jellyfish what to look and listen for, and when it happened, Jellyfish informed Blackgaard.

What was cool was the way Jellyfish informed him. Blackgaard had apparently managed to get his hands on a radiofax receiver, like the ones Western Union used in their Telecar telegram delivery vehicles back in the 1940s. Only someone had modified it for him so that when people sent him messages, instead of being typed out on paper, they would appear on his computer screen. Retro and cool at the same time. Of course, it was a direct connection—Blackgaard couldn't use it to hack into Whittaker's computer. *Which is why he needs me,* Maxwell thought. *Myron also told Blackgaard about me. That's the scary part. I can't trust anyone here.* He chortled aloud. *So what else is new? No biggie. All I have to do is make sure Blackgaard always needs me.*

Maxwell spent the rest of that week attending classes and working at the retirement home, though he stopped pilfering items at Blackgaard's insistence.

"It's too risky, Richard," Blackgaard told him. "If Mr. Glossman can catch you, so can the police. And you need to keep off the police radar for the work you will be doing for me."

Maxwell didn't like it—it meant a cut in his income—but he really didn't have much choice, since he no longer had anyone through whom to fence the merchandise. And though Blackgaard promised to pay him handsomely, he would do so only if Maxwell got results.

That was okay, though. Maxwell had another plan for supplementing his income once he got the gig as head of computer security—a plan he had formed even before he met Blackgaard. Campbell College had two shortened summer terms of six weeks each. The first term had ended the week before the warehouse trip; the second term was just about to start. The plan came to him last semester in chemistry class of all places. He didn't much care for chemistry. He understood the basics, which was good enough to get him a passing grade, but he was a prodigy at it compared to the two mouth-breathing knuckle draggers who sat in front of him.

Kenneth Ellis and Donald Pearce were the school's best athletes, and "sports" and "troublemakers" were the only contexts in which the word *best* could be applied to them. Their athletic prowess had allowed them to skate through their high school academics, and as a result, they were woefully ill prepared scholastically for the rigors of higher learning. Not that they cared; they thought their athletic abilities would get them through college just as they had gotten them through high school. But the dolts soon learned that they were actually expected to complete their assignments and earn passing grades to maintain their full-ride scholarships. Surprisingly, they were smart enough to realize they weren't smart enough, so they sought help—but, unsurprisingly, not from legitimate tutors. They turned to their less athletic alums and elicited their "assistance" via threats and payment.

Maxwell fell into the latter category. He had earned a small sum writing the jocks' term papers for English composition during spring semester. At first, Maxwell thought ghostwriting term papers might be a good way to keep making money, but writing ended up being so boring—and actually took a bit of work to accomplish—that he rejected the idea. But as he watched the two gorillas use a Bunsen burner to light afire strands of hair they plucked from their own heads in Professor Cyril's chem lab, and then noticed their shock and concern when they got back their latest test papers and saw the large Fs in red ink at the top of both, a new idea took shape in Maxwell's mind. He approached Ellis and Pearce with it after class as they sat at a picnic table under a shade tree on a grassy area of the quad, not eating their lunches.

"Hello, boys!"

Pearce just kept sitting and staring at his failed test paper, while Ellis stopped flicking his french fries at a squirrel in the tree and glared at Maxwell. "Are you lost, Max-nerd?"

"No, but I think you two are."

Pearce kept staring at his paper. "How can we be lost? We're right here."

Ellis snorted, then said, "What do you want?"

Maxwell smirked. "Looks like you guys have a little chemical imbalance."

Ellis's brow furrowed. He scanned his body and then Pearce's. "What are you talking about? We're in perfect shape!"

How thick can you get? thought Maxwell. He pointed

to Pearce's test paper. "Not with your bodies. With your grades."

Maxwell saw a lightbulb go on in Ellis's head, and the dolt snorted again. "Oh, I get it! *Chemical* as in *chemistry*. Ha! That's a good one!"

Pearce finally looked up at Maxwell. "So what if we are? What's it to you?"

Maxwell shrugged. "Oh, nothing. Just that I might be able to help you with them."

Ellis leaned forward. "Whadaya mean *help us*?"

Maxwell grinned. "What if I could guarantee you an A in chemistry?"

Pearce's eyes narrowed. "How? This ain't no paper you can write for us. This is a test. It's already done."

Ellis nodded. "Yeah, and we ain't into studying. Besides, it ain't just one test. We did this on *all* of 'em. You gonna help us with *all* of 'em?"

"And we're gonna do this on the final on Thursday, too," Pearce muttered. "You gonna help us with *that*?"

"If I can . . . Would that be worth something to you?"

Pearce pounded his fist on the table. "What do you think, dweeb? If I fail chemistry, I lose my scholarship. Of course it's worth something to me!"

Ellis, who jumped when Pearce pounded the table, swallowed hard and said, "Yeah! What he said."

Maxwell smiled and said, "Good." He turned and started to walk away, but Ellis stopped him. "Wait! You gonna help us or what?"

"Don't worry. I'll be in touch." He took a few steps, then turned back and added, "Just remember how much my help is worth to you, boys. 'Cause this time it'll be a lot more expensive than what you paid me for writing those reports." He turned again and walked away, wishing he could see the looks on their gooney faces.

Of course, to make good on his proposal to them—and now, to do what Blackgaard wanted—Maxwell needed to get the head of computer security job first. But that was just a formality. It was Thursday, and Mr. Burglemeister had summoned Maxwell for his final interview.

He fairly skipped down the quad sidewalk toward

the information technology building that housed Burglemeister's office. Though outwardly calm, he was giddy on the inside. He was so anxious to get there, get hired, and get started that he arrived at the building fifteen minutes early. *It won't do to appear too eager,* he thought, so he stopped in front of the glass entry door and checked his appearance in its reflection. *Hair—perfect; teeth—gleaming; smile—charming.* He'd even put on a tie for this, and it was expertly tied and hanging straight. He checked his watch. Fourteen minutes to go.

He sighed and looked out at the quad. A few feet farther down the sidewalk, a blonde girl with her hair in a ponytail was standing behind a folding table under a canopy, arranging flyers and information sheets on the table in front of her. Maxwell checked his watch again and then headed toward the table to see what she was selling.

The front of the table had a brightly decorated sign taped to it. At the top of the sign were the words "Mentors Wanted!" in bold, colorful letters. Beneath that, in smaller but equally bold, colorful lettering, it read, "Help shape young minds! Student counselors are needed for a special test program at CCC. Be a mentor to a gifted youngster. Make a difference!" The blonde girl thrust a flyer at Maxwell, smiled brightly, and said, "Hello! Want to make a difference?" Her teeth fairly sparkled.

Maxwell smirked and took the flyer. "Always."

"Great!" replied the blonde. "There's no better way to do it than to be a mentor to a gifted young person!"

"Is that so?" said Maxwell with feigned sincerity.

"Oh yes! These are supersmart kids from the foster-care system. They've been here on campus since the beginning of the week, and they need mentors like you to help them adjust to college."

"Mm-hmm," Maxwell grunted. "Help them how?"

The blonde cocked her head from one side to the other as she talked. Her ponytail bounced rhythmically. "Well . . . make sure they're doing their work and get to where they're supposed to be, keep an eye on them, and make sure they're included in the great stuff going on around campus . . . and, oh, just generally be

Ah! Maxwater! Right on time! Come in! Come in! Zit! Zit!" he said, ushering Maxwell into the office.

Maxwell started to correct the old guy about his name, thought better of it, and sat in one of the chairs facing the desk. Burglemeister closed the office door, quickly rounded the desk, and sat in his comfortable-looking leather desk chair. The leather squeaked, and the springs moaned as he lowered his considerable bulk into it. He smiled at Maxwell across the desk and said, "Vell, I'm sure you haf been on pins und noodles all veek about the job, yah?"

Maxwell suppressed a smirk. "Uh, yah . . . er, yes . . . er, yes, sir. That's certainly one way of putting it."

"Yah, yah, I thought zo." Burglemeister leaned back in his chair, and its springs protested the increased stress with a grinding groan. He brought his fingertips together over his ample belly. "As you know, Maxstein, decisions like zis are never simpleton. A lot of factors must be veighed, a lot of information consumed, und a lot of considerations . . . uh . . . vell . . . considered. Ve haf to make absolutely certain that ve are hiring zee

with them and there for them if and when they need you."

"Sounds like a pretty big time commitment."

"Well, yes, but a rewarding one!"

Maxwell put on a thoughtful expression. "How rewarding?"

The blonde's smile faded slightly. "I'm sorry?"

"How . . . rewarding?" he repeated slowly. "Just what do I get out of it?"

The blonde looked quizzical. "Uh, *get out of it?*"

"Yeah," said Maxwell. "Get out of it. As in, *what's in it for me?*"

The blonde's brow furrowed. *You can almost see the wheels turning in her brain,* thought Maxwell, suppressing a laugh.

She swallowed, took a breath, and said, "Uh, well, uh, you get college course credit . . . and the joy of bonding with a smart young person and helping shape his or her mind!" The smile returned.

"I see," said Maxwell as sincerely as he could, and then added, "That's it? No money or anything?"

"No, no money. It's strictly volunteer."

Maxwell nodded. "So let me get this straight. I have to spend a lot of time—*my* time—being coach, counselor, teacher, mentor, and babysitter to a brainiac urchin. And all I get out of it is a single lousy course credit?"

"Well, that, and the great satisfaction of knowing you helped shape a young mind," the blonde replied. "And making a new friend, of course." Her smile was brighter than ever. "So . . . are you interested?"

Maxwell chuckled and flicked the flyer back down on the table. "No, but I want to thank you for giving me something amusing to pass the time while I waited for my appointment."

The blonde's smile melted into a frown as Maxwell checked his watch and then turned and headed toward the information technology building's front doors.

He chuckled as he walked down the hallway toward Burglemeister's office. Some people were so gullible. She was cute, though. Maybe after the interview, he'd go back, turn on the charm, and get her to go out with him. A new job and a date—not a bad day's work.

As he rounded the corner, he saw so[mething that] made him do a slight double take. A boy, [ten] or eleven years old, was walking down the h[all to]ward him. He had short brown hair, freckl[es,] slightly upturned nose upon which perched a [pair of] oversize glasses. He wore patched jeans and wo[rn] sneakers and a small white lab coat befitting his [age,] under which Maxwell could see the triangle of a fad[ed] striped pullover shirt. The boy had a satchel of boo[ks] over one shoulder and was gnawing on a banana as he walked. He stopped at the door to the computer security room and was about to slide a keycard through a keypad next to the door when he caught Maxwell looking at him.

They locked eyes for an instant, and then the boy slid his keycard in the slot and quickly punched in the code on the keypad. The door buzzed, he opened it, and then he disappeared inside the room. The door automatically shut behind him. Maxwell frowned, then continued on toward the offices.

Mr. Burglemeister greeted him at the front desk.

right person for zis position. Choose zee wrong one, und zee whole thing is kaput!"

Maxwell was roaring with laughter on the inside, but outside he remained completely serious. "I understand, sir."

Burglemeister leaned forward. The chair squawked. "Goot. I hope zo. Because after careful und sober consternation, taking all things into account, I vanted to be zee first to tell you zat . . . you're not getting zee job."

Maxwell smiled with false modesty and opened his mouth to say "Thank you" . . . and then Burglemeister's words registered in his brain. The smile faded. "I'm . . . *not* getting the job?"

Burglemeister shook his head slowly. "No."

"But . . . but . . . *why?*"

"You vere a very strong second," Burglemeister said reassuringly. "Und you certainly haf zee computer knowledge und grades—"

"Then what—?"

"—in your *computer* classes. In your other classes, though . . ."

Maxwell's insides had stopped laughing. *This can't be happening!* Burglemeister shuffled through some papers on his desk. "Your grades und attendance in your other classes are *furchtbar*—terrible. You barely pass, und you barely show up!"

"Well, I-I can explain."

Burglemeister held up a hand. "Yah, yah, I'm sure you can. But it is still here on your record."

Maxwell opened and closed his mouth.

Burglemeister sighed heavily. The chair squeaked. "I like you, Maxleib. You know computers, und you make me haf zee giggles. But I simply cannot haf someone mit such poor academic performance in charge of computer security." He frowned sympathetically. "I'm sorry."

Maxwell swallowed. "Yeah . . . me, too," he muttered. He rose from the chair, opened the office door, started to leave, and then turned back to the desk. "Who *did* get the job?"

"Oh, uh, his name is . . ." Burglemeister shuffled through the papers again and drew one out. "Yah, here it is. His name is Eugene Meltsner." He looked up at Maxwell. "Do you know him?"

"No," Maxwell replied. "Never heard of him."

Burglemeister's eyebrows rose. "A graduate student. Excellent grades und attendance."

Maxwell scowled. "I'm sure." He walked away, leaving the office door open.

This is a nightmare! he thought, striding down the hallway toward the front entrance. *How could this have happened? I had this wrapped up. Everything was set. Then some top-student-perfect-grades-and-attendance übergeek shows up and ruins everything! Eugene. Even his name sounds geeky!*

Maxwell burst through the front doors and out onto the sidewalk. The quad had more people on it now, some hurrying to class, some strolling and reading, some lying on the grass. A small group was gathered at the picnic table under the tree where he had met with Ellis and Pearce. Maxwell scowled. *That* plan was now done. It would have been such a sweet setup too—easy money! And what was he going to tell

Blackgaard? This was bad. He growled. *Everything was great a little while ago, and now, to use Burglemeister's words, "Zee whole thing is kaput"!*

Just then he heard a familiar voice. It was the blonde at the table under the E-Z UP canopy. She was still perky, still smiling, and still trying to get gullible dupes to volunteer to be mentors to a bunch of preadolescent brainiacs. He sneered at them and shook his head. Some people were so . . .

Wait a minute! *Preadolescent brainiacs?*

He had an idea—if it panned out. A *brilliant* idea! He raced over to the blonde, who was just finishing her spiel with another student. She turned, smiling, and said, "Hi!" Then she noticed it was Maxwell and said with disgust, "Oh, *you* again."

He smiled sincerely. "Hi, again."

"Listen," she snapped, "I'm doing something very important here—something I believe in. I'm not here for your warped amusement."

He exuded charm. "I know. And I'm sorry I acted that way before. I was just about to go into a really big meeting, and I was nervous and needed to calm down. And . . . and that's no excuse for the way I behaved. Really, I'm very sorry."

The blonde's expression softened. "Well . . . okay, I guess."

Maxwell picked up a flyer. "Besides, the more I thought about it, the more I realized this is a great idea."

The blonde's smile returned in all its radiant glory. "Really?"

"Yeah! I mean, like you said, it's important."

"It *is*. It truly *is*!"

Maxwell matched her radiant smile with one of his own. "So these kids . . . they're all gifted?"

"Oh yes! Supersmart."

"And they're all over the college?"

"Everywhere!"

He leaned in slightly. "Are there any in the computer department?"

She chortled. "Sure. A *lot*, in fact."

He also chuckled. "Do you have a list of their names handy?"

She smiled even bigger. "Absolutely!" She reached under the table and pulled out a clipboard. Attached to it were several sheets of paper filled with names, small photos of the kids, and information about each of them. She handed the clipboard to Maxwell, who flipped through the pages carefully.

"Aren't they cute?" said the blonde. "I mean, when you see them, how can you *not* want to help them, right? Now the ones with the red *X* next to the picture are taken. But as you can see, there are still plenty left." She sounded as if she were selling him a car.

She said more, but Maxwell had stopped listening. He'd found it—the picture he was looking for. And there was no red *X* next to it. Perfect. He looked at her and smiled again. She fairly beamed.

He turned the clipboard around and showed her the picture. "Tell me about . . . Nicholas Adamsworth."

CHAPTER FIVE

Dear Mom,

What a week! If I ever thought camp would be boring, was I ever wrong!

So in my last letter, the girls and I were getting ready to go on a nature walk/camping trip. We loaded our gear into our backpacks in short order—or at least I did. The girls took a bit longer. I introduced them to our guide, renowned nature expert Wilma Neidlebark, a tall, stately looking woman who sometimes sounds like a man doing an impression of the queen of England. She does know a lot about nature and camping, though, and she advised the girls to pack light because "we can't be lugging around excess paraphernalia." Once she explained that *paraphernalia* means "miscellaneous articles associated with a particular institution or activity that are regarded as superfluous," and when I explained to the girls that *superfluous* means "unnecessary," the packing went a little faster.

For about thirty seconds.

Then Alison had a meltdown over not being able to watch TV; Robyn had a meltdown over how unfair it was that the boys got to do recreational and sports activities when the girls had to go on a nature hike, and why couldn't they do the same things as the boys did, and I should go talk to the camp director about letting them compete with the boys; and Donna had a meltdown over there being no place in the wilderness to plug in her hair dryer.

Again, the only girl who didn't have a meltdown

was Lucy. I did see her whispering at the cabin window with Jill Blankenship, the girl from another cabin I told you about in my last letter. That should have set off an alarm in my brain, but since Lucy has never been one to cause trouble, I didn't give it a second thought. Big mistake.

Finally everyone was all packed, the tents were rolled up, and we took off into the great outdoors. Mrs. Neidlebark really did know a lot about nature and where the most beautiful hiking trails were. She pointed out plenty of God's most marvelous creations. I know it doesn't sound all that interesting, but Mrs. Neidlebark described everything in such detail, it was really mesmerizing. It even got Alison to stop talking about TV for a while.

As it turned out, Mrs. Neidlebark's talks were a little too mesmerizing, because it was during the caterpillar talk that I failed to notice Lucy and Jill sneak away from the main group and head off into the forest. I still didn't notice it even after the talk, because it was getting dark, there was a peal of thunder, and Mrs.

Neidlebark hurried us all along to get to the campsite before it started raining. It wasn't until we had set up the tents and gotten supper started that I noticed the girls were missing.

I think you would have been proud of me, Mom. I didn't panic. I calmly informed Mrs. Neidlebark of the situation and then organized some of the other counselors into search parties. Next, I got my other girls fed and squared away in their tent. This involved convincing a panicked Robyn, who hates bugs, that the huge centipede she thought was crawling around on her sleeping bag was just her hair barette. I assured them that Mrs. Neidlebark was in the next tent if they needed anything. This made everyone happy, even Alison, who took comfort in holding on to what I thought was her Bible but turned out to be a copy of last week's *TV Guide*. Then I joined the other counselors to go look for Lucy and Jill—right as it started raining. And I didn't bring a raincoat.

It was pretty miserable out there. I was soaked to the skin, but fortunately it was a warm shower and not a cold one. We searched everywhere for the girls the whole night but couldn't find a trace of them.

Finally the rain stopped, and the sun crept up. We were dragging our way back to the campsite when who should be headed straight for us but Mrs. Neidlebark—with Lucy and Jill in tow! They had gotten back a short time after we had left and decided to play a prank on Lucy's tentmates by pretending to be the Goat Man, a silly legend in these parts.

Turns out the girls weren't lost at all. Jill knew exactly where they were. They had spent the whole time splashing in the stream under the gorgeous waterfall at Trickle Creek and then watching beautiful wild horses run at Roth's Canyon.

I don't suppose I have to tell you how I felt when I first saw those girls, Mom. It was probably the same way you felt when I was little and slipped away from you at that busy shopping center. Remember? When the policeman brought me back, you hugged me and then gave me a spanking. That's how I felt about Jill and Lucy—especially Lucy.

They were perfectly fine for the rest of the campout, no trouble at all. So I decided to wait until we got back to our cabin at camp before taking any real action. And when we arrived back here a few hours ago, I took Jill and Lucy aside. Lucy looked pretty contrite, but Jill didn't seem bothered in the least. She cocked her head at me and said, "So what're you gonna do, Connie? Throw us out of camp?"

"I should. But you're in Pam's cabin," I told her, "so it's up to her to decide what to do with you."

She smirked at me and said, "So I can go?"

"To Pam, yes."

The little imp smiled and actually said, "Terrific! See you later, Lucy." And then she scampered off without a care in the world. Lucy waved good-bye to her and then turned back to me looking very guilty. "Will Jill get sent home?"

"Probably not," I said. "Pam is only going to warn her this time."

She swallowed and said, "Will *I* get sent home?"

"Do you think you should?"

"I . . . I don't know."

"What happened, Lucy? How could you do something like that?" I was trying to read her expression, but it confused me. She seemed sorry, but there was something else in her eyes—something I had never seen from her before: a bit of defiance.

"Well," she replied, "Mrs. Neidlebark's lectures were so boring and . . . and Jill said she knew all these really neat places to go, and I . . . I *wanted* to go."

"But that's not like you. I thought you were more responsible than that."

She frowned and said, "I am . . . I think. But for once I didn't feel like being responsible. I wanted to do something different. I wanted to run off and act kinda crazy like Jill always does. She's so . . . free. Haven't you ever felt like that, Connie? Haven't you ever felt reckless and just did what you wanted to do?"

"Well—" Of *course* I had! I *knew* I had. It's part of the reason I got fired from Whit's End. But I couldn't tell her that. Instead, I said, "How I feel has nothing to do with this, Lucy. The rules are the rules. But since

Jill's not going to be sent home for this, I don't think it's fair to send you home. So I'm going to give you a warning this time. But don't let it happen again."

She looked down and said very softly, "Yes, ma'am."

"And try to stay away from Jill. I'm not sure she's a good influence on you."

"Yes, ma'am."

"You better go get your gear unpacked."

"Okay, Connie. And . . . thanks."

She turned and walked back to the cabin.

I guess I'm not much of a disciplinarian, Mom. It really hurt to have to reprimand Lucy. But letting her off with just a warning was the right thing to do, right? I mean, the Bible tells us we're supposed to have mercy and forgive . . . so why don't I feel very good about this? Believe it or not, I actually asked myself what Whit would do. And I think I know.

Oh, well, hopefully that will be the end of it, and there won't be any more problems. We have a competition to prepare for, after all!

I'd better close now, Mom. I need to go unpack

too, and do my laundry, and take a shower. I hope everything is okay with you and the town. You really haven't seen Eugene around at all? Again, if you do, tell him I said hi.

I miss you!

Love,

Connie

CHAPTER SIX

"What do you mean you didn't get the job, Richard?"

He can even sound intimidating on a speaker phone, thought Maxwell. A chill went down his spine. He was sitting in Glossman's office on Sunday afternoon. The councilman sat across the desk from him, and Blackgaard's voice, cold as death, came out of a small black box on the desk between them. "You assured me that it was in the bag."

"I thought it was," said Maxwell evenly.

"Then what happened?"

"Someone named Eugene Meltsner happened."

"Meltsner?" said Glossman. He suddenly looked very uncomfortable.

"You know him, Philip?"

"Yes, sir. He used to work at Whit's End—one of the employees Whittaker fired because of the Applesauce incident."

"I thought that was a girl—Katie or Kelly or—"

"Connie, sir. Connie Kendall. She was the other one he fired."

Maxwell noticed tiny beads of sweat appear on Glossman's upper lip and forehead. Interesting. Aloud he said, "I applied at the beginning of the week, and the department secretary said no one else had applied." He looked at Glossman. "But somehow between the time I applied and the end of the week, Meltsner got the idea to apply."

Glossman shifted in his chair.

"Why would the department head choose him over you, Richard?"

Now it was Maxwell's turn to squirm. "Well . . . I really don't know. I mean Burglemeister told me I was the front-runner in my first interview with him. Then when I went back for the final interview, he told me he was hiring Eugene." Glossman was smiling now. Maxwell added, "I sure wish I knew how he got the idea to apply."

Glossman's smile faded. "Who cares? The point is, he has the job—and you don't."

"That's right, Richard. I was counting on you, and you let me down. I don't like to be let down, Richard."

Maxwell smirked. "I'm sure you don't, Chief. And that's why I haven't let you down."

"Explain."

The smirk became a grin. "Just because I didn't get the head of computer security job doesn't mean I didn't get any job."

Glossman's eyes narrowed. "What are you talking about? What other job did you get?"

The grin was now a smile. "Congratulate me. You're looking at"—he nodded at the speaker—"and talking to the student counselor and mentor of one Nicholas 'Nicky' Adamsworth."

"Who in the blazes of earth's great fiery sun is Nicholas 'Nicky' Adamsworth?"

Maxwell chuckled. "Oh, he's just a supersmart, eleven-year-old kid who is part of a new state program that places gifted kids in college."

A chuckle came from the speaker.

Glossman blinked blankly. "I don't get it. So?"

"Do try to keep up, Philip. I take it little Nicky has been placed in Campbell College's computer department, Richard?"

"Oh yeah . . . in the security room."

The speaker nearly jumped off the desk when Blackgaard laughed. "Excellent! But can you control him?"

"Not a problem. I've already got him working on a project for me."

Glossman held up a hand. "Wait. Just so I'm clear here. You're saying you're gonna get this Nicky kid to use the school's high-tech system to hack into Whittaker's computer? Isn't that adding to our security problem?"

Maxwell leaned back and talked as though he were explaining something to a child. "No, Councilman, Nicky's not gonna do the hacking. I'm going to use Nicky's security clearance to get access to the school's high-tech system so I can hack into Whittaker's computer." He smirked at Glossman, who glared back at him.

"Well done, Richard. Just the kind of resourcefulness I'm looking for."

"I know. Thanks."

"Please keep us informed of your progress. And now, if you don't mind, I need to talk to Philip privately."

"Oh, uh, sure." Maxwell rose from his chair. "I'll be in touch, Doctor. See you around, Councilman." Maxwell crossed to the office door, opened it, stepped outside, and closed it behind him. He then made sure his footsteps could be heard as he walked down the hallway and the stairs.

On the landing, he stopped, waited a few seconds, heard Glossman's door open slightly and then close again, then tiptoed as quietly as he could back up the stairs and down the hallway to Glossman's office. The truth was, though he was sure he could control Nicky—he'd already gotten the kid to access Ellis's and Pearce's grade files—the boy was also being very protective of his security keycard. Maxwell knew he could push the kid only so far. He also knew the councilman had it in for him. He needed an extra advantage, and to get that, he needed information. He crept up to the office door, leaned in close, and heard the somewhat muffled conversation inside.

"He's gone, sir."

"Good. What is the status on the building?"

Glossman took a deep breath. "Unchanged, sir."

There was a long pause.

"You did hear me tell Richard how I don't like to be let down, didn't you, Philip?"

"Y-yes, sir, but—"

"I don't think I have to remind you how important this is, do I?"

"No, sir. It's just that Mansfield Computers has an ironclad three-year lease. He doesn't care about utility increases or surrogate charges. He's making too much money."

"Excuses, Philip? Are you going to lose me another building in Odyssey?"

"N-no, sir!"

"I thought I could trust you to handle this."

"You can, sir!"

"Then handle it, Philip."

Maxwell heard all he needed to. He crept back down the hallway and the stairs, and this time he exited the building.

Mansfield Computers in Gower's Landing shopping center? What did Blackgaard want with that place? Was he actually thinking of coming to Odyssey? And why did that name—Mansfield—sound so familiar? Maxwell knew he had seen it before, but where?

He was sure it wasn't at school. And the only other place he went to was—

It hit him. The Odyssey Retirement Home. *That* was the connection! But how would that help him?

Unless . . . A plan formed in his brain. He'd need to do a little snooping to make certain there was a connection between Mansfield and the home. But if it was there, the plan might just give him the advantage he needed.

He smiled.

Incompetents! I'm surrounded by incompetents.

Blackgaard hung up the speakerphone and fumed. Patience was never one of his virtues, he knew. Old Professor M had always told him that. *You are brilliant, Regis,* he would say, *perhaps my most brilliant student. But you must learn patience. That has been the downfall of many great men. Learn patience.* Then again, look what patience had gotten the old man. He'd been sick, feeble, wheelchair bound, within reach of his goal, only to fail miserably and die.

"I will not fail," Blackgaard growled.

Yet there was something to the old professor's words. The wheels had been set in motion; he had no choice but to wait and see if Glossman and Maxwell could get them to their destination. "They'd better," he growled again. "There's too much at stake."

He opened the drawer of his polished oak desk and extracted a leather-bound note folder, his initials embossed in gold across the front. There was so much to do, so much yet to come.

He opened the folder and scanned his notes. When the time was right, he'd need to talk to Smitty. The proper chemicals were vital. He'd also need to pressure his contacts at the Department of Defense. They'd be reticent, but with the information he had on them, they'd come around. And then there was European security and his "friends" in the Middle East. That would be the most dangerous part of all. But if he could bring it all together, make it all work . . . "It will be more than worth the aggravation," he muttered, "and the danger."

The key was Applesauce. And that meant getting a foothold in Odyssey—which brought him back to Glossman and Maxwell. The dolts. If they only knew what was really going on here. He felt his frustration rise again.

He rose from his leather executive chair and crossed the lushly carpeted floor to a painting on the wall opposite his desk. The painting depicted a beautiful forest glade through which ran a serene stream. The stream meandered in and out of the woods but was painted in such a way that if you looked closely and traced it carefully, it actually led to a waterfall that became a crystal-clear pool, which, in turn, fed the stream that meandered through the glade—a never-ending cycle. He stared at it for a long moment and felt, if not peace, then a sense of calm. That would do.

The painting was attached to the wall on a hinge. It opened like a cupboard door. He swung it away from the wall to reveal what it hid: a safe. He dialed the combination deftly, heard the tumblers click, cranked the handle, pulled open the door, and removed the only thing inside.

It was a fragment of an extremely old piece of paper, encased in a clear plastic bag. This is what was really going on here; this was why he needed the Fillmore Recreation Center, a stronghold in Odyssey, and Applesauce. He had tracked Professor M halfway around the world, enduring deprivation, disease, and hardship, before finally catching up with him in the jungles of South America. All for this fragment—or, more precisely, what was written on it.

Scrawled on the paper in shaky handwriting were ancient words in a language he did not know and could not read. Fortunately, Professor M had translated them before he died. What the words said were unbelievable. But the old professor swore they were true. The fragment was so old, Blackgaard didn't dare remove it from the bag, but he ran his fingers over the plastic, imagining he could feel the power of the words through it.

His fingers stopped at the bottom of the fragment,

where the most astounding words of all were written, words that made him believe the professor was right. There was no need to translate them; they were written in English, in the same handwriting as the ancient language above them. Three clear words:

"John Avery Whittaker."

CHAPTER SEVEN

Although Eugene had been in the computer department at Campbell College many times, he had never been nervous about it before. Then again, he had never been hired to work there before. He was also rather surprised at how fast the hiring process had been. After his conversation with Philip Glossman at Mansfield Computers, he had decided that perhaps the councilman was correct, and he needed to explore his options. Not that he desired to be beholden to Glossman, of all people, but he was secretly grateful for the information about the job opening in the computer department. He really didn't want to work in a computer store. He felt the duties there would have been far beneath his skill set in computer technology and far above his skill set in sales.

So after pondering the pros and cons, he decided to give it a go, and he applied for the job with Mr. Burglemeister the next morning. He was just in time. Mr. Burglemeister told Eugene that he was the last applicant for the position. The department head had all but made the final decision on filling the position with the previous applicant. Eugene left the preinterview believing that he had not gotten the job, but that afternoon he got a call from the department secretary asking him to come to the office immediately. When he did, Mr. Burglemeister hired him on the spot. The last time he had been hired that fast was . . . well . . . at Whit's End.

Eugene felt a pang of remorse thinking about his former job and his former employer, but he didn't allow the feeling to go any further. He needed to focus on the task at hand. It had been five days since he was hired, and today was his first day on the job, even though it was the first week of the second, shortened, summer semester. Mr. Burglemeister was giving Eugene a guided tour of the college's computer facilities, much of which Eugene had already seen. Their first stop was the student lab, a sterile, white room with rows of computers humming and whirring, in front of which sat a variety of students typing away at their keyboards and occasionally whispering or talking in low voices, sometimes to each other, and sometimes to themselves. There was no rule about not talking while in the lab, but for some reason everyone treated it as if it were a library.

Eugene and Mr. Burglemeister exited the lab into the hallway, and Mr. Burglemeister pointed out several rooms as they passed them, describing their functions and the work that went on in them.

". . . und zat room is zee college's general data-processing department where information about zee students are put into zee computers—names, addresses, zat sort of thing."

Eugene nodded. "I understand."

Burglemeister motioned toward the next door to their right. "Now, if you come zis way, I'll show you something *really* special!"

They strolled down the hallway, and Eugene cleared his throat. "Mr. Burglemeister, I hope I've made it very clear how much I appreciate the college hiring me."

Burglemeister waggled a finger at him. "Tut, tut, Hubert."

"Eugene."

"Yah, yah—your records show you are one of our best graduate students. Mit your computer experience, I should be thanking *you* for taking zee job. Ve must make sure ve are hiring zee right kind of people to verk for us. Ach! Here ve are!" They stopped in front of a door. Unlike all the other doors, this one had no window in it or sign on it. It also had on the wall next to the doorknob a keypad with a card slot. "Zis is our computer security division. You'll notice zat zee door is always locked. You'll haf your own keycard. Zis room is *sehr* top secret. *Die meisten* confidential."

Eugene frowned. "Top secret? Why?"

"Zese computers contain all our financial information, student grades, und reports. Ve can't haf just *anyone* poking their eyes around in it."

"I see," said Eugene thoughtfully. "Very impressive."

Burglemeister slid his keycard through the slot and punched a code into the keypad. The door buzzed, he pulled it open, and they went inside. The door automatically shut behind them. Like the computer lab, this room was also sterile and white, but unlike the lab, it was empty and completely quiet except for the mild electronic hum of the computers. Burglemeister stopped and closed his eyes blissfully. "Ahhh . . . listen."

Eugene stood perfectly still, straining to listen. Oddly enough—or perhaps not, when he thought about it—the sound reminded him of the computer room at Whit's End. But he said aloud, "What am I listening for?"

"*Nichts!* Nothing! Zat's zee point. In zis room, you haf zee joy of peace und quiet. Ah, vat I vouldn't give to be vere you are."

Eugene's brow furrowed. "Where am I, sir?"

Burglemeister opened his arms wide. "Here! Zis is vere you'll be verking! Ve're putting you in charge of our high-security programming!"

Eugene's jaw dropped, and he blinked several times. "You're putting me *in charge*? Nothing was said to me about being in charge!"

Burglemeister scratched his head. "*Nein*? Hmm! Must've slipped my mind. But why shouldn't you be? Your records show you're a near genius mit computers."

"Near?"

"*Ach*! How I envy you!" Burglemeister sighed. "Zee solitude, zee programming . . . no loud people, no noise but zee gentle hum of zee *elektronik*. It should be quite a relief after verking at—vat vas zee name of zat kids' place, Hubert?"

"Eugene. It was called Whit's End."

"Yah, yah, zat's right: Mit's End. You can put zat nightmare behind you. You'll enjoy zis job. Just computers und computer programs. *Wunderbar!* No more screaming children surrounding you mit clutter und distractions. *Absoluten* paradise."

Eugene sighed sadly. "Yes . . . paradise."

Suddenly, a throat being cleared very loudly invaded the peace of the computer hum. "A-hem!"

Eugene looked around. "What was that?"

Burglemeister also looked. "I'm not sure. It sounded like—"

A quiet male voice said, "Over here, sir."

Burglemeister turned and smiled. "*Ach meine sternen!* Nicholas! Sorry, I didn't see you sitting over zere! Nicholas, come over here und meet Hubert Meltsdip."

Eugene watched as a small, freckled boy wearing a white lab coat emerged from behind a computer workstation.

Eugene extended his hand. "Eugene Meltsner, actually. Pleased to meet you."

"And zis is Nicholas Appleworm."

Nicholas peered up at Eugene through dirty, over-sized glasses and took his hand. "Uh, Adamsworth. Hello, Mr. Meltsner." They shook.

"Please, just call me Eugene, uh, Nicholas."

Burglemeister beamed. "Nicholas vill be verking for you. He's part of a special test program zee college has started for *jugendliche*—er, children—mit extremely high intelligence. He's proven himself to be quite goot mit computers—so goot, in fact, ve put him in here. Don't let his age fool you."

"How old are you, Nicholas?" Eugene asked.

"Eleven years, three months, two days, ten hours, and fifty-four minutes old," Nicholas replied instantly. "Not counting daylight savings."

Eugene smiled, impressed. "Eleven years old! I didn't start my college studies until I was thirteen."

Nicholas nodded. "You know what it's like, then."

"Oh yes. But at that time, they didn't have advanced study programs like this, and—"

"*Ach*, I'm sure you *wunderkindern* haf a lot to talk about!" Burglemeister interrupted. "Und I'll leave you to it. Hubert, if you haf any questions, don't hesitate to call."

"Thank you, Mr. Burglemeister. I won't."

"*Auf Wiedersehen*, Nicholas. Don't dillydally too long. Remember, zee study program depends on *you*."

"I won't forget. Good-bye, Mr. Burglemeister."

Burglemeister clapped them both on the shoulders affectionately, beamed again, and then left the room.

Eugene chuckled. "Well. He seems competent enough."

Nicholas shrugged. "He's all right . . . for someone with his IQ."

"What did he mean when he said the program depends on you?"

"This is a test program for some of us kids in the foster program. My parents died when I was little." He pushed his enormous glasses higher up on his nose. "Anyway, they started this program to see if kids my age with my intelligence can adjust to college life. They say I've got the brains for it, but not the body. It's not exactly elementary school around here."

"Is the program working?"

"I hope so. If we fail, they'll cancel the program, and then we'll all be stuck."

"All?"

Nicholas nodded. "Yes. Me and kids like me. We'll go back into the system, which means going back to regular school. Then I'll spend most of my time trying to keep from being picked on. A lot of kids are barbarians when it comes to us geniuses."

Eugene frowned. "Oh yes. I remember those days."

"At least in college, they leave me alone." Nicholas gestured around the room. "Here, I can *try* to fit in . . . as well as I can fit in anywhere, I suppose. Sometimes I'm not sure I ever will. That's why they put me way back here. They don't know what else to do with me." He put his hands in his lab-coat pockets. "I overheard Mr. Burglemeister say you used to work at some sort of amusement shop for children. That must've driven you crazy!"

Eugene sighed. "No, actually now that you mention it, it's the only place I ever thought I fit *in*." The pang of remorse returned, and this time he let himself experience it for a few moments. He really did miss Mr. Whittaker and Whit's End—and even Miss Kendall, though he'd never admit it to her. He felt the sadness welling up inside him and then noticed that Nicholas was staring at him. He took a deep breath and said, "But enough of this sentimentality. I would be grateful if you would introduce me to the computer operations here, Nicholas."

Nicholas smiled from freckled ear to freckled ear. "My pleasure! Come right this way."

CHAPTER EIGHT

A few days later, Eugene received an interesting request via e-mail from Mr. Burglemeister, though he didn't realize just how interesting it was at the time. The request itself was rather routine; what was interesting was Nicholas's reaction to it. Eugene found the boy sitting at his usual workstation in the computer security room.

"Salubrious salutations, Nicholas."

The boy grinned at the greeting. "Hi, Mr. Meltsner!"

"As I've been telling you for the last two days, Eugene will be sufficient."

The grin became a smile. "Okay, Eugene. How may I help you?"

"Now that I have the hang of the computer system here, Mr. Burglemeister has sent me an e-mail asking me to do a random check on the students' grades."

Nicholas's smile faded. "A random check?"

"Yes. He wants to make sure they're being put into the computer correctly. We would certainly hate for a student who received an A to accidentally get a C in a class."

Nicholas shifted uneasily on his stool. "Do you think that's absolutely necessary? Wouldn't it be better to . . . to wait for the student to complain?"

Eugene shook his head. "Mr. Burglemeister said he wants this department to have a reputation for accuracy. Complaints from students would give the wrong impression of our work."

Nicholas licked his lips. "But you shouldn't have to do that. I'll do it."

"It's quite all right, Nicholas. Why should I give you the boring work?" He turned to go to his station.

Suddenly Nicholas jumped off his stool and grabbed the sleeve of Eugene's lab coat. "I don't mind. Really! Let me do it, Eugene. Please!"

Eugene looked at his sleeve and then at Nicholas, who quickly let go and dropped his hand. Something wasn't right here. During the past two days, he had found the boy to be brilliant, friendly if somewhat timid, and very eager to please—but not *this* eager. "Nicholas, is everything—"

Just then, there was a loud knock at the door, so loud they both jumped and turned. "Hello? Who could that be?" Eugene said.

Despite being startled a second ago, Nicholas now looked relieved. "Oh, that'll be Richard Maxwell. He's my counselor here at the college." He crossed the room to the door.

Eugene blinked. "Counselor?"

"He's in charge of me—a student-counselor, of sorts. He's the one who has to tell the college how I'm doing."

Nicholas twisted the knob and pushed open the door, and in sauntered Richard Maxwell. The door auto-shut behind him. "Hey, there, Nicky, what's happening?"

"Hello, Mr. Maxwell." Nicholas tried to smile, but Eugene thought it looked more like a grimace. Maxwell chuckled.

"'Mr. Maxwell.' You crack me up, kid." He ruffled Nicholas's hair and then noticed Eugene. "Oh! You must be Eugene Mellnerd."

"Meltsner."

Another chuckle. "Yeah, sure. You're the bum who got my job."

"I beg your pardon?"

Maxwell strolled into the room as if he owned it. "You got my job. I was all lined up to work in here until you applied."

Eugene's mouth dropped open. "You were going to work in here?"

Maxwell stopped next to Nicholas's workstation and ran his fingers lightly across the keyboard. "Sure! Computers are my area of expertise, as they say—that and a good game of pool."

Eugene's brow furrowed. "I'm slightly confused. I thought you were a counselor."

Maxwell smirked. "I am. I'm a lot of things at this college. I'm whatcha call a *Renaissance man.* Okay with you?"

"I suppose so." *There is something familiar about this person,* Eugene thought, *but I can't place my finger on what it is.*

Maxwell leaned back on the workstation table and crossed both his arms and legs. "You used to work in town, didn't you? For that Whittaker guy. Whit's End. He has computers there—or were you cleaning high chairs for him?"

Eugene stiffened. "Computers . . . inventions . . . I did a variety of work for him."

"What happened? Get bored?"

"No. I had a run-in with a computer program called Applesauce."

Maxwell looked amused. "Applesauce, huh? What kind of run-in can you have with a program called Applesauce?"

"It was a special program that—" Eugene stopped himself. *Why am I telling him this?* Aloud he continued, "I am quite certain that is no one's business but my own."

Maxwell uncrossed his arms and held up his hands in mock surrender. "Hey, no problemo. Just making conversation. I wanted to stop in and make sure you're not overworking Nicky, that's all."

Nicholas had been so quiet, Eugene had almost forgotten he was there. He turned to the boy. "I'm not overworking you, am I, Nicky—I mean, Nicholas?"

"No, sir." The boy's eyes shifted rapidly back and forth between Eugene and Maxwell, who uncrossed his legs and stood.

"Good. That's all. Take 'er easy." He crossed to

the door casually, opened it, and then looked back at Nicholas. "I'll . . . be talking to you later, kid."

Nicholas nodded. "Yes, Mr. Maxwell."

"*Mr. Maxwell . . .* You crack me up." He chuckled and exited. The door auto-shut behind him.

Eugene frowned. "Well, all I can say is counselors certainly have changed since I was an undergrad."

Nicholas took a deep breath and returned to his workstation. "H-he's okay. He's actually pretty smart."

Eugene's eyes narrowed. "He's not treating you badly, is he?"

"No, no, sir!" said Nicholas a little too quickly.

Something is definitely not right here, thought Eugene. Nicholas was behaving oddly, and there was, indeed, something familiar about Maxwell, but he just couldn't pinpoint what it was.

Eugene decided to put it in the back of his mind and let his subconscious deal with it for a while. He took a breath and said, "Well, we should get back to work. You have data to enter, and I have grades to check!"

Nicholas licked his lips again. "A-are you sure you don't want me to do that?"

"Positive. You just keep doing what you were doing before Maxwell came in."

The boy looked as though he were about to argue again, but then he sighed and said, "Yes, Mr. Meltsner."

"Again, it's just Eugene," he said with a smile.

Nicholas nodded, smiled weakly, then climbed back onto his stool.

CHAPTER NINE

Eugene spent the next few hours poring over grade sheets and computer records from the previous semester. He had found no discrepancies and considered reporting back to Mr. Burglemeister that the entire exercise had been both fruitless and pointless. He decided to examine one last grade sheet before giving his bleary eyes a break. He opened a folder labeled "Chemistry 101—Professor Cyril." His eyes flitted back and forth between the paper and the screen. Nothing. Nothing. Nope. Nothing. No—

Wait.

There *was* something on this one. "This is most curious," he muttered. He picked up the telephone and punched in an extension. The speaker in the receiver chirped twice and clicked, then a female voice said, "Data entry. This is Anne."

"Hello, Anne. Eugene Meltsner here in computer security. Could you please bring in your reports about a student named"—he squinted at the screen—"Kenneth Ellis? I believe his grades were entered on the fifth of the month."

"Ellis . . . Kenneth . . . Got it. Okeydokey. I'll be right in."

"Thank you."

Eugene placed the receiver in its cradle and stared at the grade sheet again as Nicholas walked up.

"What's wrong, Mr.—Eugene?"

"I was double-checking students' grades, and I found one that doesn't match."

"Doesn't match?"

Eugene pointed to his computer screen. "Look. According to the computer screen, Kenneth Ellis got an A in his chemistry class. But"—he held up the gradesheet folder—"according to this report here, he got an F. He failed it."

There was a soft knock at the door. Eugene rose and quickly crossed the room. "This might help."

He opened the door, and Anne, a cute, young dataentry person, poked her head in and shoved a file toward him. "Here's that report you wanted, Eugene."

"Thank you, Anne." He took it from her, she retreated, and he let the door auto-shut behind him. He riffled through the file's pages as he made his way back to his desk. He found the sheet he wanted and scanned it quickly.

There it was again. "Aha! According to this report, the grade was entered as an F."

Nicholas swallowed hard. "M-maybe somebody made a mistake."

Eugene frowned. "How? After the grade was entered

into the computer last month, no one was supposed to touch it. It was input as an F then, and it should be an F now. Yet it isn't . . . see? The computer now clearly shows that Kenneth Ellis got an A."

"Maybe there's a bug in the system."

Eugene scratched his head. "Hmm. I don't think so. Unless, of course, the teacher had made a mistake and then asked for the grade to be changed." He thought for a moment, then closed the file, plopped it on his desk, and said, "I'll be back in a little while, Nicholas. I'm going to find Kenneth Ellis's chemistry professor."

And before Nicholas could respond, Eugene crossed the room in three strides, pushed open the door, and headed down the hallway toward the building entrance.

Eugene crossed the quad to the science building, where Professor Cyril's office was located, only to discover that he had left several minutes earlier to teach a class.

Eugene then went to the professor's normal classroom, where a sign on the door said that Cyril's class had been moved to room 408 in the social sciences building across campus.

Eugene raced from the building and headed after him, hoping to catch him before he reached his destination. He wasn't disappointed. The professor—mid-fifties and balding, with a full, graying beard—wore a herringbone jacket with leather patches on the elbows and black-framed, thick-lensed glasses. He was toting a heavily laden book bag toward the social sciences building as Eugene ran up to him. "Professor Cyril! Professor Cyril!"

Cyril stopped and turned to Eugene. "Yes? What is it, young man?"

Eugene grabbed at the stitch in his side and gulped in air. "I've been . . . looking for you . . . all over . . . campus."

"Mmm," the professor grunted. "That's because they scheduled my lectures all over campus. No respect after all these years."

"Do you . . . have a minute? I must ask you . . . a couple of . . . questions."

"My office hours are posted on my office door. See me then."

He turned to go, but Eugene stopped him. "No, sir, you don't understand . . . I'm not one of your students." He finally caught his breath. "I work in the computer security division here at the college. I need to ask about one of your students."

Cyril's eyebrows raised. "Oh! You'll have to come to my office then. All my records are there. Which student?"

"Kenneth Ellis."

The professor sneered. "Ellis! What's he done now?"

"You remember him?"

"You'd better believe it!" Cyril nodded. "Nothing but a troublemaker. There were two of them—Ken Ellis, and what was his name? . . . Pearce! Yes, Donald Pearce. That's it. Ken Ellis and Donald Pearce. Two of a kind. Barely came to the lectures, and when they did, they made a mess of everything. Cracking jokes, spoiling experiments, lighting afire strands of their hair, releasing hydrogen sulfide in the lab. Those two are hard to forget."

Eugene wrinkled his nose at the thought of the rotten smell of hydrogen sulfide. "Do you remember what Ellis's final grade was?"

The professor snorted. "Ha! That's easy. An F. What else *could* I give him? Gave Pearce an F too."

"So you *distinctly* remember giving Kenneth Ellis a failing grade?" Eugene said insistently.

"I just said so, didn't I?" Cyril snapped. "Look, you'll have to excuse me. My next class is in that building over there, and up four flights of stairs." He moved off, muttering, "This'll be a lot easier when I get tenure."

Eugene called after him. "Thank you, Professor! You've been a big—" But Cyril was gone. "Uh . . . help." Eugene frowned, then turned and headed back to the information technology building, deep in thought. *Well, now, this is turning into quite a mystery.*

Eugene slid his keycard into the slot outside the

computer security room, then punched in the code. The door buzzed, he turned the knob, pushed the door open, and entered. It auto-shut behind him. Nicholas was at his workstation but stopped working when Eugene entered. The boy watched as Eugene made a beeline to his own desk and computer. Eugene sat and began typing rapidly on the keyboard.

Nicholas said, "Did you find out anything about Kenneth Ellis?"

"Yes." He kept typing and muttered, "Donald Pearce . . . Donald Pearce . . . Donald—There it is. Donald Pearce."

Nicholas slipped off his stool and approached Eugene. "Donald Pearce?"

Eugene nodded. "Professor Cyril, the chemistry teacher, said he definitely gave Kenneth Ellis a failing grade, but it's here on the computer as an A. The professor also happened to mention that he gave Donald Pearce a failing grade too. Pearce and Ellis were both in the same class. Real troublemakers, apparently. And I want to double-check to see if—" He stopped typing suddenly. "Yes. There it is! Just as I suspected. It says here that Donald Pearce got an A in that chemistry class as well. There's definitely something going on here."

Nicholas shrugged. "Another mistake?"

Eugene shook his head. "I don't think so." He turned to the boy and said animatedly, "Nicholas, do you see what this means? Somehow someone got into this computer system and changed Ken Ellis's and Donald Pearce's grades!"

Nicholas swallowed hard. "A hacker? Do you think someone's tapping in from the outside?"

"Possibly. But I don't know how." Eugene leaned back in his chair and crossed his arms. "This system is supposed to be foolproof against anyone but authorized personnel getting into it." His hand went up to his chin, and he scratched it gently.

Had Eugene been looking at Nicholas, he would have noticed the boy's complexion had paled. "Maybe it's an odd coincidence, Mr. Meltsner. Maybe it's no big deal. I-I wouldn't spend a lot of time thinking about it."

Eugene kept staring at the screen and stroking his chin. "I don't agree. If someone knows how to change two grades, then what's to stop them from changing four . . . or twenty . . . or hundreds? I've read of students charging a lot of money to change failing grades to passing ones."

Nicholas laughed nervously, "Heh-heh . . . at Campbell College? Be careful, sir, not to let your imagination run away with you."

Eugene stopped scratching his chin, looked at Nicholas, and nodded. "Yes . . . you're right." He leaned forward in his chair. "I have to think clearly about this. There must be a way to find out who is doing it—and why." His eyes narrowed. "And that is precisely what I'm going to do." He started typing furiously again.

Nicholas's eyes were as wide as saucers. He licked his lips, backed away slowly, and returned to his workstation.

CHAPTER TEN

Dear Mom,

I had to send Lucy home from camp today.

Dear, sweet, gentle, kind, considerate, obedient Lucy Cunningham-Schultz blatantly defied the rules again—even more seriously this time than before. I can't believe it. I also can't believe I had the courage to follow through with such a severe punishment.

Here's what happened: I spoke to the camp director,

and he agreed that the girls should get the chance to compete with the boys at recreational and sports activities. So my girls competed against the boys in cabin 7 in a contest involving archery, canoeing, and a relay race. Those two cabins contained the kids from Whit's End: Jack, Jimmy, and Oscar against Donna, Robyn, and Alison. Lucy was the substitute for my cabin, and they made me the announcer for the whole competition.

Now I didn't know that Robyn and Donna had gotten so fed up with Alison's obsession over TV, and Alison had gotten so fed up with Robyn's and Donna's obsessions with clothes, hair, and makeup, that they made a deal. Robyn and Donna would stop talking about how they looked if Alison would stop talking about TV.

It seemed to work—for a while. The boys won the archery contest because Jimmy distracted Robyn right as she was about to shoot, and my girls won the canoeing competition because the boys forgot to untie their canoe from the dock. They were all even going into the relay race. In this relay, each runner had to wear a hat upside down. Inside the first runner's hat was an egg. The first runner had to go halfway around the track to the second runner, then move the egg from the first hat to the second hat *without* touching anything or breaking the egg. The second runner then had to do the same with the third runner. Whichever team got to the starting line first without breaking its egg would win the whole competition.

It was a close race right up to the last handoff. But Alison had trouble getting the egg into Robyn's hat—mainly because Robyn was concerned that the egg would drop and break on her new jogging shoes. Unfortunately, she said this out loud to Alison, who was so happy to have won the no-talking-about-clothes-and-TV agreement that she actually *did* drop the egg—which broke on Robyn's new jogging shoes! It looked like the boys would win everything. But Oscar dumped their egg into Jack's hat so hard, it also broke and ran down the side of Jack's face.

So no one won the competition. Coach Zachary and the camp director decided that because the boys weren't exactly good sports throughout the competition, they needed to spend a little quality time scrubbing floors and washing windows. Meanwhile, back in my cabin, there were plenty of feelings to sort out: Robyn and Donna were mad at Alison, who was elated that she hadn't caved first, and so she could now yammer to her heart's content about TV again. I reminded everybody that first and foremost, we should treat each other with love. They all admitted they had forgotten that point.

I also reminded Alison about the Bible verse in Philippians, where it says, "Whatever is true, whatever is noble, whatever is right, whatever is pure, whatever is lovely, whatever is admirable—if anything is excellent or praiseworthy—think about such things." I told her that a good way to stop being so obsessed with television was to fill her head with good things like Bible verses instead of silly things like the latest TV shows. She agreed to try.

The only one I didn't have a problem with was Lucy. Or at least that's what I *thought*.

See, while everyone was focused on the crazy competition, Jill and Lucy made plans to meet up after lights out again. Everyone was pretty tired after the events of the day, so Lucy had no trouble sneaking out of the cabin. The odd thing was that once outside, she and Jill didn't really go anywhere. If they had, they might not have been caught. Instead, they stood between the cabins and talked, and that's where Mrs. Neidlebark nailed them. She blew her whistle, which jolted me out of a sound sleep. I rushed outside and there they all were.

Mrs. Neidlebark left the girls—and their fates—in my hands. I took them to the great hall and talked with the camp director privately about what they did. He told me he would back whatever decision I made.

I went back out to the girls and asked what they had to say for themselves. Lucy said nothing, but Jill piped right up. "Look, Connie, she went out because of me. If you're gonna punish anybody, it oughta be me."

I told Jill that was very noble of her, but that's not the way it worked. She retorted with probably the worst thing she could have said right then: "So what're you gonna do? You're not gonna send us home for something so dumb, are you?"

That pretty much made the decision for me. "Yes," I said, "I have to send you *both* home from camp. I told you on the first day what the rules were, and you broke them. I'm going to tell the camp director to call your parents. They'll pick you up as soon as they can get here."

Jill didn't take that very well. First she thought I was kidding, and when I told her I wasn't and that she should go pack, she blew her stack—and surprisingly, not just at me.

"I don't believe this! I've *never* been sent home from camp! See, Lucy? This is what happens when you do it your way. Neidlebark never would've found us in the shelter. Nice going!"

She stormed off. I asked Lucy what Jill meant by "the shelter." She told me it was an old air-raid shelter by the lake that was built in the 1950s. "That's the reason I was outside," she said. "To tell Jill that I wasn't going with her to see the shelter. And that I liked being crazy and having fun sometimes, but I had to do what's right." She paused, and I think she expected me to say it was okay and she could stay. Instead, I said, "But you didn't do what's right. You disobeyed the rules."

I could see that surprised her. Her mouth opened, then she said, "B-but I . . . I was keeping us from—"

"You disobeyed the rules, Lucy. Campers aren't allowed outside the cabins after lights out. I'm sorry. I really am. But I'm responsible for you, and I have no choice. You better go pack too."

Her mouth closed tight, and she glared at me and said in a cold voice, "Yes, ma'am." She started to go, then stopped and added, "And I'm sorry for hurting you." Her voice was still cold, and I got the impression she wasn't really sorry at all.

"It really does hurt, you know," I said.

"Yeah," she said, "I know."

I nodded and said, "See you back in Odyssey."

She left without another word.

It was the toughest thing I've ever had to do, Mom.

And I was completely serious about how much it hurt. Just like you always said when you had to spank me: "This hurts me a lot more than it'll hurt you." Remember? Now I know how that feels. And I understand how much it must've hurt Whit when he had to fire me. And maybe I even understand a little better how God must feel when He has to discipline all of us.

Anyway, that's what I learned at Camp What-A-Nut this week. Not bad, huh? Hope your week was better than mine. I need to go now. See you soon.

Love,

Connie

P.S. If you see Whit, tell him I said hello.

CHAPTER ELEVEN

The following day, Eugene raced to the office, fumbled with his keycard, botched the code twice, finally got it right, then burst through the door. Nicholas was already at his workstation.

"Is everything all right, sir?"

Eugene smiled. "Nicholas! I'm glad you're here. I've had a breakthrough!" He crossed the room to his desk and plopped down in his chair.

"Breakthrough, sir? About what?"

Eugene began typing. "About the grades discrepancy. I feel so foolish that I didn't think of it sooner!"

Nicholas slid off his stool and slowly approached Eugene. "I . . . I need to talk to you, Mr. Meltsner."

Eugene continued typing but glanced at the boy with slight frustration. "Eugene. The name is Eugene." He returned his gaze to the computer screen. "I was thinking about it last night before I went to sleep. Suddenly it dawned on me: the *computer* can tell me *when* the grade changes were made! Right down to the exact day and time. It keeps a thorough record of everything that happens when it's on. I'm running the program now. This will tell me all I need to know, and then maybe we can track down the culprits."

Nicholas took a step closer. "That's what I have to talk to you about, Mr. Meltsner. You see—"

Eugene ploughed ahead, barely listening. "I must remember to tell Mr. Burglemeister what a wonderful job he did when he designed this system. It was ingenious of him to—" The computer dinged.

Eugene's eyes widened. "There it is, Nicholas!

Right there!" He pointed at the screen. "Anne originally entered the grades for Kenneth Ellis and Donald Pearce on the fifth. And then . . . on the tenth at two thirty in the afternoon and again at two thirty-four, they were changed right here in this room. Someone did it *here*. Who was working that day, Nicholas? Do you remember? Check the log."

Nicholas paled. "I don't need to check the log, sir. I know who it was."

"You do? Who was it?"

Nicholas looked as though he was about to be sick. He swallowed slowly, took a deep breath, and said, "Me."

Eugene frowned. "You were here?"

"Yes, sir."

"You mean you were actually here in this room when someone changed the grades?"

Nicholas shook his head. "No. I was here alone."

"Then—"

"Don't you understand?" the boy blurted out. "*I* changed the grades! *Me!* That's what I'm trying to tell you. I changed the grades."

Eugene sat back in his chair, his body numb, trying to comprehend what Nicholas had just said. "You changed the grades . . . but . . . why?"

Nicholas turned away. "Would you believe me if I said Mr. Burglemeister told me to?"

"*Should* I believe you?"

"No."

Eugene leaned forward, put a hand on the boy's shoulder, and said gently, "Why did you change the grades, Nicholas? That was . . . illegal. It was wrong."

Nicholas bowed his head. "I know it. But I had to. He made me."

"*Who* made you?"

At that moment there was a knock at the door. Eugene and Nicholas looked toward the entrance, and Nicholas crossed to it. "That'll be Richard Maxwell."

Eugene scowled. "Maxwell? What does he want *now*?"

Nicholas opened the door, and Maxwell strolled in as casually as he did the first time. "Hey, Eugene. Hiya, Nicky. What's going on?"

Eugene rose from his chair. There was still something oddly familiar about this person. "We're terribly busy right now, Richard. Can you talk to Nicholas later?"

Maxwell smirked and looked at Nicholas. "Maybe. How 'bout it, Nicky?"

Nicholas looked up at Maxwell, paler than ever. "He knows."

Maxwell's smirk dissolved. "*Who* knows?"

The boy jerked his head toward Eugene. "Eugene knows about changing the grades."

Maxwell's jaw hardened. "You blabbed. I told you to tell him   "

"He wouldn't have believed it," interrupted Nicholas. "He would have checked with Mr. Burglemeister."

Maxwell scowled and then smirked again. "You got a big mouth, kid."

Eugene felt as though he were walking through a thick fog. He stared at Maxwell, trying to focus. "*You're* the one who put Nicholas up to this? You made him change the grades?"

Maxwell patted Nicholas on the head. "That I did, Hubert. That I did."

"But . . . he's just a *child*! Why?"

Maxwell sauntered around the room, pausing briefly at Nicholas's workstation, and then ambled to the desk and sat in Eugene's chair. "I told you. I'm a Renaissance man. I dabble in lots of things." Maxwell put his feet on the desk. "Particularly moneymaking kinds of things. With Nicky in here, and students all over the campus willing to pay to have their grades fixed, how could I pass up the opportunity?"

"But . . . but that's . . . *dishonest*!"

Maxwell put his hands on his chest and gasped mockingly. "*Really*? I didn't realize! Guess I should stop it, huh?"

Eugene threw up his hands. "Of course you should! Nicholas, how could you do this?"

Nicholas bowed his head again. "I-I couldn't help it."

Maxwell chortled. "Look, Huey, don't start in on the kid. He really didn't have a choice."

"Everyone has a choice!"

"Yeah, well, Nicky didn't." Maxwell locked his fingers behind his head and smiled.

Nicholas looked up at Eugene, tears welling in his eyes. "He said he'd give the college a bad report about me. He said he'd make them put me back into the system if I didn't change the grades."

Eugene was horrified. "He can't do that! You could've just told on him!"

The boy squeezed his eyes shut. Tears trickled down his cheeks. "I . . . I was afraid to."

Maxwell unlocked his fingers and leaned forward in the chair. "You see, Brain Boy, as his counselor, I decide what happens to him here. And if he told, they'd still send him back. Like I said, he didn't have a choice." He sniffed. "And neither do you."

Eugene scoffed. "I beg your pardon? I think I do."

Maxwell shook his head. "Nope. You tell on me, and I'll tell on Nicholas, and he'll be history at this college."

"You wouldn't."

"I would," said Maxwell.

"He would," said Nicholas.

Maxwell stood and crossed to the door. "So that's your situation, Houston. What's it gonna be? Tell and ruin Nicholas's life? Or keep your mouth shut and let us all live happily ever after?"

He turned the knob and opened the door. "Well? What's it gonna be?"

After Maxwell left, Eugene and Nicholas spent the rest of the afternoon in silence, quietly going about their work. Eugene felt sick. He had agreed not to tell on Nicholas, and his stomach was rebelling at the dishonesty. But try as he might, he didn't really see what else he could do. He sighed heavily. He was used to scientific problems—problems that were actually solvable using hard science, and solvable to the satisfaction of all parties involved. Moral dilemmas were foreign territory for him. He wished he had paid closer attention to Mr. Whittaker. *He* would know how to handle this situation.

At six o'clock, Nicholas finally broke the silence. He slid off his stool and walked over to Eugene's desk. "Eugene?"

"Yes, Nicholas." He didn't look at the boy.

"It's six o'clock. Don't you think it's time to leave?"

"No. Not yet. I'm thinking."

"Oh." Nicholas inched closer to Eugene's line of sight. "I . . . I have to get back to my dorm room."

Eugene swiveled his chair away from Nicholas's gaze. "Go ahead."

"But . . . I feel bad," said Nicholas pleadingly. "I don't want to leave if you're going to stay."

"Don't worry about me." Eugene swiveled his chair so he couldn't see the boy at all.

Nicholas sighed. "All right, if you're sure. Good night, Eugene."

"Good night, Nicholas."

The boy turned, went back to his workstation, and gathered his things. He took a step toward the door and then said, "Thanks for not telling."

Eugene still didn't look at him. "I'd rather you

didn't mention that. Ever again. I'd like to pretend it never happened."

"Yes, sir." Nicholas crossed slowly to the door and was just about to open it, when Eugene suddenly sat straight up in his chair. "Wait a moment! That's it!"

Nicholas started. "What? What's it?"

Eugene swiveled around. "Pretend it never happened!"

The boy's brow furrowed. "Huh?"

"That's what we need to do!" Eugene popped up from his chair. "Nicholas, what would stop us from going back and fixing the grades?"

"Going back and—"

"Yes! Computers can do that. We'll simply undo what you did!" He crossed to the boy. "Do you remember whose grades you changed? There couldn't have been that many."

Nicholas shrugged sheepishly. "Well . . . actually . . ."

Eugene blinked, surprised. "Really? Then there's no time to lose. Sit down." He took the boy's book bag and ushered him to the desk. "I want you to write down all the names you can remember and what their original grades were in which classes. Can you do that?"

Nicholas sat. "I-I think so. But what about Richard Maxwell?"

Eugene smiled. "That's the beauty of it. What can he do if the grades are correct? What proof will he have? And if he tries to get you thrown out of school anyway, I'll fight it. I can fight for you if there's no evidence against you, correct? You'll be making amends. Hurry! The sooner we get this done, the better!'"

It was very late when Eugene finally finished correcting the grades. Nicholas had long since fallen asleep at the desk chair, and Eugene, himself weary and bleary eyed, had to almost carry the boy back to his dorm before making his own way home.

As soon as Eugene and Nicholas were out of the building, Maxwell emerged from the shadows in the hallway and sidled up to the security room door. He produced from his pocket a keycard with the name "Nicholas Adamsworth" printed across the front.

Nice to know I can still lift a keycard, he thought, and smiled. *And good thing for me they were both so tired, they didn't notice I took it. Extreme fatigue always leads to carelessness.* He snorted, slid the keycard through the slot, and punched in the code he had memorized from observing both Nicholas and Eugene entering it, admiring his own memory prowess. When the door buzzed, he pushed it open and stepped inside.

Maxwell crossed quickly to Nicholas's workstation and typed in the security code. "Nicky, you really need to be more careful with your security codes," he chuckled softly. After a second, the computer beeped, and the word *Ready* appeared in the upper-left corner of the screen, followed by a flashing cursor. He took a deep breath, muttered, "Here we go," and typed ":\\Search\WhitsEnd\Mabel\Applesauce\".

The machine whirred.

Maxwell smiled.

CHAPTER TWELVE

The next morning, Eugene awoke to the phone ringing. At first he thought he was late for work, but then he remembered he didn't have to be there until later that morning. So who would be calling at this hour? He sat up, shook the cobwebs out of his head, and lifted the receiver. "Greetings and salutations. Eugene Meltsner speaking."

"This is Delores from Mr. Burglemeister's office

calling," said a nasal voice on the other end. "Mr. Bur-glemeister would like to see you here immediately."

"Oh, uh, well I just awoke, and—"

"Immediately." The line clicked and then went dead.

Eugene took a deep breath and exhaled slowly.

This is not good.

He showered and dressed as fast as he could and then raced to the campus, across the quad to the information technology building, and inside to Mr. Burglemeister's office. Delores buzzed her boss on the intercom. "Mr. Burglemeister?"

"Yes, Delores?"

"Humont Milner here to see you, sir."

Eugene grimaced and said, "That's Eugene. Eugene Melts—"

"Send him right in."

"Yes, sir." Delores released the intercom button, looked at Eugene disapprovingly, and nodded toward the office. Eugene rounded her desk and moved toward the door, each step feeling as if he were slogging through mud. At the door, he stopped and knocked softly. He heard a muffled "Enter!" and opened the door.

Mr. Burglemeister sat behind his desk. Gone was the friendly demeanor that greeted him the first time they spoke. This time the old gent was all business. "Come in, Hubert—er, Eugene. Please, sit down."

Eugene sank into a chair. "Thank you, sir. I came as soon as I got your message."

"Goot of you."

Eugene swallowed—or tried to. His mouth had suddenly gone dry. "Uh, how may I help you?"

Burglemeister peered over his spectacles at him, took a deep breath, and frowned. "Zis is difficult for me, Eugene. Actually, I'm in a state of disbelief. But . . . I haf become aware of some very illegal activities going on here at our college."

"Illegal?"

"Yah. Our campus security has uncovered a racket zat involves changing students' grades for money."

"Really?" Eugene's voice cracked.

Burglemeister nodded. "Ven I found out about it, I did zee only thing I knew to do. I began monitoring zee activities of your department. Yesterday, to be exact."

Eugene paled. "Y-yesterday?"

"Yesterday. My report shows a very heavy concentration of activity—especially last *nacht*. You vere zere late last night, veren't you, Eugene?"

"Yes, sir."

"Vat vere you doing?"

"Um, work?"

"Vat kind of verk?"

"Just . . . ver—er, work."

Burglemeister lifted a paper from his desktop and scanned it. "My report shows vat kind of verk you vere doing. You vere changing students' grades. Am I correct?"

The jig was up. But, oddly, now that it was, Eugene felt very calm. He looked straight at Burglemeister. "Yes, sir."

Burglemeister dropped the paper and then interlaced his fingers and rested his elbows on his desk. "Unless you haf a plausible explanation for why you vere changing students' grades mitout authorization, I can only conclude zat you are part of zee plot to change grades for money."

"That is understandable, sir."

Burglemeister put his hands on his desk, pushed himself out of his chair, and sighed deeply. "Oh, Eugene, Eugene!" He paced around his desk. "I had such high hopes for you! As it is, you're going to haf to appear before zee college board of inquiry. Zey vill decide vat to do mit you." He slumped against his desk.

Eugene lowered his head. "I understand." *Just tell him!* "Mr. Burglemeister . . ."

Burglemeister leaned forward. "Yes, Eugene? You vant to say something? *Was ist es?*"

No! You can't! If you do, it will hurt Nicholas. He exhaled and said, "Nothing, sir. I have nothing to say."

Burglemeister nodded slowly and looked very old. "*Sehr gut*, very well." He stood, went back to his chair, and sat down heavily. The chair springs groaned. He laced his fingers together again and rested his chin on them, staring down at his desk. Without looking at Eugene, he said. "Zee board of inquiry vill meet zis afternoon at *drei uhr*—three o'clock—in President's Hall. Do not be late, *bitte*—please. Zat vill be all."

Eugene rose slowly and went to the door.

Then Burglemeister said, "*Eins* zing more." Eugene turned back, but the old gent was bent over his desk. Without looking up, he said, "I vill need your keycard."

Eugene slowly took his keycard from his pocket and placed it on the desk in front of Burglemeister. He then sighed, walked back to the door, opened it, and left the room.

CHAPTER THIRTEEN

The rest of the morning and early afternoon dragged by. Eugene stayed to himself. Since he couldn't go to the computer security room anymore, he holed up in the library. But even books couldn't comfort him today. He found an isolated cubby and hid from the world.

At last it was time. He made his way across campus to President's Hall. It looked not unlike a courtroom, austere and solemn. Eugene sat at a small table directly in front of a long table with three conference-room chairs behind it. Delores, Mr. Burglemeister's secretary, was already there, prepared to take notes. She sat at a side table. After a few moments, a door behind the long table opened, and three gentlemen walked in. Eugene recognized two of them. First was Dr. Thomas Grayson, the tall, graying, sharp-nosed college president, who sat in the center chair. Next came a plump, round-headed man Eugene didn't know, who sat to the president's left. Bringing up the rear, to Eugene's great surprise, was Mr. Whittaker. He sat to the president's right. Once they were all in their chairs, Dr. Grayson pulled a microphone toward himself and blew into it.

"Testing . . . one . . . two . . . three . . . Is this tape running?" He apparently got the okay from an unseen audio engineer, cleared his throat, and continued. "The Campbell College Board of Inquiry is now in a closed session. I am Dr. Thomas Grayson, president of the college. To my left is Ralph Harris, member of the board of trustees. To my right is John Avery Whittaker, also a member of the board of trustees. Thank you, gentlemen, for coming on such short notice."

He put on a pair of reading glasses and passed folders from a small stack in front of him to Mr. Harris and Mr. Whittaker. "You'll find all the pertinent information and computer reports from Mr. Burglemeister in these folders. Sorry about the formality, but they want it to sound good on tape. Mr. Whittaker, I believe you have had some past experience with Mr. Meltsner here?"

Whit nodded. "I have, Dr. Grayson."

"Then maybe you can give us some insight at this hearing. Eugene?"

"Yes, sir."

Dr. Grayson took off his glasses. "It's important you understand that we are not a court of law. Our purpose here is to assess the charges against you and pass on a recommendation to the College Disciplinary Committee. In this case, we will decide whether to expel you from school . . . or to perhaps even have you arrested. Do you understand?"

"Yes, sir."

"Do you have anything you wish to say?"

"No, sir."

Grayson's brow furrowed. "What you're being accused of is *very* serious. Don't you have *anything* to say in your defense?"

"No, sir."

"Nothing at *all*?"

"No, sir," Eugene said stoically. "I was in charge of the department. The responsibility is mine."

Grayson considered Eugene for a moment and then said, "Hold on a minute, please. I need to confer with my fellow board members." He rolled his chair back away from the microphone and motioned for Harris and Whit to join him. The three of them spoke in hushed voices for several moments, and finally Grayson motioned for them to resume their places. He said, "The board of inquiry will take a short recess for . . . ah, a conference. Sit tight, Eugene." He turned to Harris and muttered, "Let's go, Ralph. There's coffee down the hall. Delores, care to join us?"

The three of them exited through the back door. Whit stood, put the folder on his chair, and rolled it around the board table and over to Eugene's table, where he placed the folder on the table and sat. "Well. Hello, Eugene. Fancy meeting you here."

"Greetings, Mr. Whittaker. I didn't know you were on the board."

Whit nodded. "Have been for quite some time. If it helps the college, I'll do it. So, you want to tell me what this is all about?"

"It's in the report. Mr. Burglemeister caught me red-handed."

"Uh-huh. And I'm supposed to believe that you're involved in some scam to make money by changing students' grades?"

Eugene stared straight ahead. "According to the report, yes."

Whit leaned in. "Eugene, look at me." Eugene slowly turned and met Whit's gaze. "Is it true?"

Eugene took a deep breath. "My department is my responsibility, Mr. Whittaker. If there is one thing I learned from you, it's to take responsibility. Or did I misunderstand you?"

"No, Eugene, you didn't. But I'm having a hard time believing you're really behind this."

Eugene cocked his head. "Why? You fired me for activity of this nature. Remember? I broke into Applesauce."

Whit leaned back. "Yes, I did fire you. And I'm glad you brought that up. You know, earlier today we questioned two of the students whose grades were changed."

Eugene shifted in his chair. "Y-you did?"

"Mm-hmm." Whit opened the folder and read from the top page. "Kenneth Ellis and Donald Pearce. Do you know what they told us?"

"No."

Whit scanned the page. "They admitted they paid someone to change their grades . . . but it wasn't you. As a matter of fact, neither of them had ever even heard of you. They said they paid someone named Richard Maxwell to do it. Quite a bit of money too."

"Oh."

Whit closed the folder. "Now, how about the truth."

Eugene looked at the table and slowly shook his head. "I-I can't, Mr. Whittaker."

Whit leaned in, placed his hand on Eugene's arm, and squeezed it gently. "Eugene, please. This is very serious. Your whole future is at stake."

Eugene took a deep breath and looked at his former employer. "Not only mine," he said softly. "Please, Mr. Whittaker, let me do what I have to do. I ruined your relationship with Connie. Let me try to do *something* right."

Whit let go of Eugene's arm and leaned back in his chair. Suddenly the front-entrance door burst open. Whit and Eugene both jumped up as Nicholas rushed in, red faced and breathing hard. "Eugene!"

"Nicholas? What are you doing here?"

"I've been . . . looking for you . . . all over the building," he panted.

"You're supposed to be in the computer security room."

"I was, until Mr Burglemeister told me what happened." Nicholas stepped closer and grabbed Eugene's shirt. "You can't do this! I won't let you do this!"

Eugene gently removed the boy's hand. "Go back to work, Nicholas. It's too late."

"No! It can't be!" Nicholas suddenly noticed Whit. "Who are you?"

"I'm John Avery Whittaker. Who are you?"

"Nicholas Adamsworth. Are you in charge of this kangaroo trial?"

Whit chuckled. "I might be."

"Then you have to stop it! You're making a mistake. I don't care if they send me back."

Eugene put his hand on the boy's shoulder. "It's all right—"

Nicholas wrenched away. "He didn't do it, Mr. Whittaker! Eugene had nothing to do with it. I'll tell you everything. I promise. Just don't let Eugene get in trouble. Please!"

Whit looked at Eugene and then back at the boy. He nodded slowly. "All right, Nicholas. Maybe you'd better start talking, then. Have a seat."

The boy took a deep breath. "Well, it all started when they made Richard Maxwell my student-counselor—"

CHAPTER FOURTEEN

Once Nicholas had finished his testimony, Whit called in the other board-of-inquiry members and shared it with them. Upon hearing it, things immediately kicked into high gear.

Dr. Grayson contacted campus security. The guards found Maxwell in his dorm room and escorted him to President's Hall. He sauntered in, as calm and unperturbed as ever, looking around absently at the room's architecture and decor as he stood next to Eugene and Nicholas. The odd sense of familiarity again came over Eugene when Maxwell stepped up next to him—what *was* it?—but he put it out of his mind again. The board members conferred privately for several minutes on their rulings about the trio standing before them, then resumed their places at the table. Dr. Grayson pulled the microphone closer and said, clearly and sternly, "Richard Maxwell."

Maxwell raised his hand and smiled. "Yo! What can I do for you, your highness?"

"On the recommendation of this board of inquiry and as president of the college, I hereby expel you from this institution for your participation in the grade-changing scheme."

Maxwell put one hand to his chest and the back of the other hand to his brow. "Oh dear! Oh my! I'm crushed. I'm heartbroken." He then chuckled at his fake anguish.

Grayson was not amused. "I'm also strongly recommending that you not get into any other college in this state."

Maxwell shrugged. "Doesn't matter to me. I've got a better job lined up anyway."

Grayson leaned forward. "Consider yourself fortunate that we aren't pressing charges with the police." He nodded toward Whit. "You have Mr. Whittaker to thank for that."

Maxwell smiled at Whit. "Oh, I'm grateful, your holiness."

Grayson scowled and then said, "Nicholas Adamsworth."

The boy stepped forward. "Y-yes, sir?"

"For *your* participation in this illegal activity, the board recommends that you be placed on indefinite probation . . . here at the college."

Nicholas's eyes brightened. "You . . . you mean . . . you're not sending me back to the group home?"

Grayson smiled slightly. "We're not sending you back."

For a moment the boy lost all intellectual composure. He smiled broadly, leaped in the air, and yelled, "Yippeee!" Then he caught himself and settled back into his reserved stance, though he still smiled broadly. "I-I mean thank you, sir. I am extremely grateful."

Grayson and the other board members stifled their amusement, and Grayson's stentorian tone returned. "Eugene Mel—ah, Melts—uh—"

Eugene stepped forward. "Meltsner, sir."

Grayson nodded. "Exactly. Because of your participation in the grade-changing scheme, willingly or unwillingly, we are relieving you of your position here at the college and placing you under the supervision of a member of our board of trustees."

Eugene's brow furrowed. "I . . . I beg your pardon? I'm not sure I understand. You're firing me?"

Grayson shook his head. "Not exactly. We're transferring you. You will finish your graduate internship where it started."

"But . . . that was at . . . Mr. Whittaker?"

Whit smiled. "Eugene, based on the sacrificial way

I've seen you behave today, I would be pleased if you would come back to work at Whit's End."

Eugene glanced around the room, leaned in toward Whit, and said in a low voice, "But what about App—?"

Whit held up his hand. "I think you've learned your lesson. I think you've learned it very well." He turned his hand over and held it out. "Will you come back?"

Eugene rose to his full height, straightened his shoulders, smiled broadly, and said, "Mr. Whittaker, I would be proud and honored to offer my meager ministrations as your most obsequious—"

"Just say yes, Eugene."

"Yes, Eugene."

Grayson looked from person to person and then nodded and said, "This meeting is adjourned."

Nicholas cheered and clapped. The board members rose and shook hands, and Grayson and Harris departed through the back door. Whit rounded the table and walked up to Eugene and Nicholas, who had stopped clapping long enough to hug Eugene around the waist. "Yay! Thanks, Eugene!"

"You did it, Nicholas. Thank *you.*"

"Congratulations to you both," said Whit. "Now maybe things can get back to normal!"

The three of them continued to talk happily, taking little note of Richard Maxwell, who had strolled toward the front door.

He smirked and muttered, "I wouldn't count on it, Mr. Whittaker. I wouldn't count on it at all."

PREVIEW OF BOOK THREE

Dr. Regis Blackgaard exploded with fury.

"Expelled, Richard? You got expelled from Camp-bell College over a lousy grade-changing scheme?" The speakerphone on Philip Glossman's desk distorted with the volume of the outburst.

Maxwell winced at the sound and stared across the desk at Glossman, who leaned back in his office chair, his arms crossed over his potbelly, and smiled blissfully at the verbal lashing Maxwell was receiving.

"I thought you were smart, clever! But apparently you don't even have any common sense! Why would you do something so idiotic?"

Maxwell shrugged. "Hey, you cut off my extra income from the retirement home, remember?"

"You've jeopardized this operation for a little extra income?"

"I didn't jeopardize—"

"You could have been arrested! You could have attracted police attention—"

"But I wasn't and I didn't, thanks to Whittaker. I knew he'd convince them not to get the police involved." Maxwell smirked. "He's a goody two-shoes like the rest of them—the biggest one of all, in fact. He's all about giving people second chances."

Blackgaard's voice turned deadly. "Well I am not about giving people second chances, Richard."

Maxwell suppressed the chill that went down his spine. He opened his mouth to respond, when Glossman leaned forward and cut in. "Of course, the worst part in all of this is that you didn't get Applesauce. You didn't even try. And now you won't be able to." He leaned back and smiled once again.

You're just loving this, aren't you, Councilman? Maxwell thought. *Well, see how much you love this.* He sniffed and said aloud, "Actually, I did try."

Glossman's smile evaporated. The speakerphone sat silent. Maxwell tapped on it and said, "Hello? Did we lose you there, Doc?"

"You tried to download Applesauce?"

"Yep."

"And? What happened?"

Maxwell shrugged again. "I couldn't do it from that computer."

Glossman leaned forward and put his hands on the desk. "Wait a minute. Back at the warehouse, you said you could do it on that computer."

"Maybe," Maxwell retorted. "I said maybe I could do it. Turns out Burglemeister may be a coot, but he's no dope. He knows his stuff. He wrote in a subroutine that notifies him when the system is being used for purposes other than those for which it was designed. I had to cover my tracks, so I hid what I did under what Meltsner was doing. That's how Burglemeister nailed him for changing the grades back."

"But you still got caught." Glossman sneered.

"Yeah, well, I thought I had better control over little Nicky," Maxwell replied. "Who knew? The point is, I couldn't have used that computer. I'm gonna need a dedicated computer with its own access, and a secure, private place to operate it from." He stared at Glossman. "Assuming, that is, that we'll actually get such a place. How's the Gower's Landing shopping complex acquisition coming, Glossy? Mansfield Computers still givin' you fits?"

Glossman's face reddened and contorted with rage. He popped out of his chair and started for Maxwell. "You slimy little sneak! I oughta—"

"Sit down, Philip!" Blackgaard said in a cold, hard voice.

Glossman stopped and gaped at the speakerphone, then slowly sank back into his chair. Maxwell was impressed. How did Blackgaard know Glossman had jumped up? Did he have a video camera in this office?

Maxwell restrained himself from glancing around the room as Blackgaard continued.

"He's right. We still don't have the building secured. And now, apparently, we're going to need it more than ever."

Glossman tugged at his collar. "I'm meeting with Webster again tomorrow, sir. We'll do everything we can."

Maxwell chuckled. "So far that hasn't been much." Glossman started to rise again, but Maxwell put up his hands. "Sorry—cheap shot. Listen, boys, I think I can help you out here."

Glossman scowled. "You think— "

"Quiet, Philip. Do go on, Richard."

Maxwell grinned and winked at Glossman, whose face reddened again. Maxwell rose from his chair and paced the room. "Before I came here today, I stopped by Odyssey Retirement Home."

"Stealing from them again?" said Glossman with a sneer.

Maxwell chuckled. "Oh, no, no. Nothing like that. I just wanted to say hi to some of the old folks there, particularly someone named Mary Hooper. Sad case, really. Her family put her in the home when her husband died. Easy to see why: she's not a very nice person. She's grouchy, snippy, and downright mean most of the time—even to kids like my sister's friend Donna. The family put Mary in the home because they don't want her living with them. I don't blame them. I wouldn't want her living with me, either. She sort of made up with her daughter a few weeks back, but I can tell you firsthand that Mary Hooper does not like her son-in-law, in the least."

There was a low growl from the speakerphone. "Getting bored, Richard. Is this going somewhere?"

Maxwell slid back into his chair and smiled at Glossman. "While I was at the home, I checked the records. Y'know, they really need to improve their security on those things. I mean it's private information, after all—"

"The point, Richard!"

Maxwell leaned in toward the speakerphone. "Mary Hooper's son-in-law—the one who doesn't want her living with him—is Bob Mansfield, owner of Mansfield Computers."